Hi, I'm
Katie Hooper

by Jane Sorenson

illustrated by Kathleen L. Smith

STANDARD PUBLISHING
[s|u]® Cincinnati, Ohio

24-02936

All Scripture quotations are from the *Holy Bible: New International Version,* ©1973, 1984 by the International Bible Society. Used by permission of Zondervan Bible Publishers and the International Bible Society.

LIBRARY OF CONGRESS
Library of Congress Cataloging-in-Publication Data

Sorenson, Jane.
    Hi, I'm Katie Hooper/by Jane Sorenson; illustrated by Kathleen Smith.
       p. cm.–(A Katie Hooper book; 1)
    Summary: When they learn that their remote Colorado cabin is going to be sold by the owner, Katie Hooper and her family set out to look for a new home.
    ISBN 0-87403-486-8
    [1. Family life–Fiction. 2. Moving, Household–Fiction. 3. Colorado–Fiction. 4. Christian life–Fiction.] I. Smith, Kathleen, 1950- ill. II. Title. III. Series: Sorenson, Jane. Katie Hooper book; 1.
PZ7.S7214Hi 1988
[Fic]–dc19
                                88-6397
                                  CIP
                                  AC

To Laura McCollough

a girl in Iowa I've never met
who wrote to encourage me
to "keep writing"

A Breakfast Picnic

I wasn't really awake. I do remember hearing the shutter squeak softly just before it banged against the window frame. And inside the loft, next to my bed, there was a thumping sound. Ignoring the thumps, I pulled the blanket up over my head. Then I relaxed. Everything was absolutely quiet.

Suddenly, I sat straight up. I pulled out the flashlight I keep under my pillow and flicked the switch. Mickey Mouse's face grinned at me. His yellow gloves pointed to five after five.

I grabbed the alarm clock. "Oh, no," I whispered. "I forgot to pull out the button."

My dog's tail thumped against the floor. Only the tail moved. The dog it was attached to lay still, so still that he could have been an old sweater. "It'll be OK, January," I told him. "If I hurry, we can still make it."

I didn't need light to get dressed. I simply put on the same clothes I took off when I went to bed. I really am supposed to wear clean underwear, but my mother never checks any more.

January was quiet. Except for his tail, he didn't even wiggle the entire time I was getting dressed. His tail gave an occasional thump. That's all.

"OK, let's go," I told him.

I had just begun backing down the ladder when my brother's door opened. "Is that you, Katie?" he whispered.

"Oh, no," I whispered. "Jason, did I wake you?"

"What does it look like?" my brother replied.

"I'm sorry," I said. "I tried to be quiet. Honest."

"It's OK. Forget it," Jason said. "You'd better hurry."

I was slowed down because I had to help January down the ladder. Personally, I've always believed he could climb down alone, but apparently he doesn't think so. He won't even try.

When we finally got to solid ground, I glanced toward my parents' bedroom. The door was still closed.

I nearly forgot my backpack. I had filled it last night and put it next to the door, but somebody must have moved it. I know I never left it on the piano.

Luckily the front door didn't squeak. I could breath easier once we were outside. By now it was no longer pitch dark out.

Well, right off the bat, my stupid dog took off after a squirrel. "This way, January," I called. My voice sounded louder than I thought it would. "Dumb dog," I muttered. "If we're late, it will be your fault."

But when we reached the shed, I saw what I was hoping for all along – my father.

Dad is a giant of a man, so naturally he wears these huge jeans. This morning, he was also wearing a hat. His hair is thinning, and he thinks if he wears a hat, people won't notice. Personally, I don't think he fools anybody.

Anyhow, Dad was looking underneath our 4-wheel drive. Only we never call it that. To the Hoopers, it is known affectionately as "Purple Jeep."

As soon as my father saw me, he straightened up. "Good morning, Valentine," he said. "I was afraid I'd have to leave without you."

"I'm sorry, Dad." I explained what happened.

"Is your mother awake?"

"I don't think so," I told him.

"Good," he said. "She didn't sleep well again last night."

January had already jumped into the back seat of Purple Jeep. He sat there waiting with his tongue hanging out.

"January's the silliest dog we've ever had," Dad laughed. "OK, let's hit the trail."

As soon as we got to the end of our lane, Dad reached into a paper bag. "How about some breakfast?" He handed me my favorite—a liver sausage sandwich.

"Any pickles?" I asked.

"Sorry," he said. "I couldn't find any."

"Jason probably ate them," I said.

As we rode along, my hair kept flying all over the place, and I had to keep pushing it out of my face. I munched happily, "Any dessert?"

"You bet!" I watched Dad grin. He reached into the sack and produced two Hershey bars. "Our favorite," he said. "Right?"

I nodded agreement as I tore the wrapper.

* * * * * * * *

Purple Jeep is ancient, and it rattled along on the unpaved road. To be honest, it even rattles on paved roads. Well, suddenly there was a loud noise. My father swerved to one side, stopped the motor, and climbed out.

"What happened?"

"Somebody shot Purple Jeep," Dad said.

"Those crazy hunters!"

I knew he was kidding. Everybody in Colorado knows you can't hunt purple jeeps in the summer.

When I turned to watch Dad, I noticed January in the back seat. "Brave dog," I told him. He poked his head out from under the army blanket. I giggled.

"It's just the muffler," Dad said, as he climbed back in. "Anyhow, we're nearly there."

We rattled and banged along until we came to a rocky stream. Dad made a right turn. Several hundred yards farther, he pulled over and parked.

"We made it. And not a minute too soon," he said. "Look, Katie! See how everything almost glows! In fifteen minutes the lighting will be perfect."

"Do you ever get tired of painting mountains?" I asked. But even as I heard my voice I knew it was a dumb question.

"Haven't so far!" Dad was grinning. He was already setting up his easel. "Katie, the only thing better than being here at sunrise is having you come along with me!"

"I'm glad I didn't oversleep," I said. I started to pull my backpack onto my shoulders. "Want me to take January with me?"

"Please do," Dad said. "Your mother doesn't

think it's safe for you to wander around alone."

I looked at January and laughed. "Some watchdog!"

My father laughed, too. "Well, a stranger wouldn't know that. Where will you be?"

"I thought I'd climb Flat Rock," I said.

My father nodded. "Fine," he said. Humming softly to himself, he began arranging his colors and brushes.

"See you later," I said. But Dad wasn't listening.

To be honest, there was no point in my hanging around any longer. My huge father, his hat still in place, was moving gracefully from side to side as he squinted at the sunrise on the mountain.

"Come on, January!" I started up the path. The dog trotted along at my side. When I looked back and waved a few minutes later, my father wasn't even watching.

January's Adventure

I walked for about fifteen minutes. I didn't even talk to January. I really wasn't thinking about anything in particular. Sometimes it's nice just to enjoy life.

My brother Jason always tries to figure everything out all the time. I mean, he even thinks he knows why people do things. In my own case, *I* don't even know why I do things, so how could my brother know? Anyhow, who cares!

"OK, January," I said. "Time for a drink." He just looked at me with those brown eyes.

I stuck my tongue out and pretended to pant. "Look, January!" I said. "How about a drink of water?"

It was no use. When I started climbing down

the rocks toward the water, he perked up. Except he thought we were going swimming!

"Look, January!" I kneeled down, cupped my hands, and filled them with water. He just sat there without moving. He watched while I drank—which took a while. I decided that next time I'd remember to bring a cup.

Well, I certainly wasn't going to hold water in my hands for any dog! "If you're that dumb, you can just be thirsty," I told January. Apparently that got to him. He stood up, wandered to the water's edge, sniffed twice, and started drinking.

"Good dog!" I said. "Good dog!"

By the time we climbed up Flat Rock, I was hot. The first thing I did was take off my backpack, and the second thing was take off my sweater.

Then, just when I felt like talking, January discovered butterflies. I watched him bound after first one and then another.

Slowly I unbuckled my backpack and reached inside.

"It's about time you let me out!" Audrey said. Audrey is my Cabbage Patch doll.

I set her down on the rock and frowned. "Audrey," I told her, "if you're going to be a pill, I may stick you back inside!"

"Ha!" Audrey said. "Just try it!"

"Don't tempt me," I told her, and I reached inside the backpack again.

"Whew! Thank you very much!" said Gomer. Gomer is a spineless stuffed lamb with more personality than some people I know.

"You are entirely welcome," I said, turning to include Audrey. "Isn't this a beautiful day?" Even Audrey had to agree.

"Now, class," I said, as my imagination really began to roll, "has anybody seen B. B.? He's been absent all week." I wasn't exactly sure how this suddenly got to be a classroom, but it really didn't matter.

B. B.'s name is really Bronco Bob. He is a souvenir from when some of Dad's friends went to a football game in Denver last year.

Well, it turned out that B. B. had been sick with strep throat. But when I reached into the backpack, he was miraculously cured.

"Did you bring your written excuse?" I asked B. B. "Strep throat is nothing to sneeze at!" I giggled.

Well, I got tired of playing schoolroom after a while—just about the time I tried to explain fractions. Gomer caught on right away, and B. B. is a whiz at math. But Audrey wanted to know which pieces were included when you bought 1/7 of a chicken.

I sat back and took a deep breath.

"Colorado is God's country," I told the dolls. Actually, I'll have to check with my father to see if that is really true. My brother Jason says I'm gullible. That means I tend to believe whatever people tell me.

"Of course, the whole wide world is really God's country," I continued. Audrey and B. B. listened carefully. Gomer never really looks at you, so with him you never can tell.

"Why, did you know there are places that don't even have mountains?" I asked the dolls. "My own parents grew up in a state that doesn't even have hills! Of course, I've never been there. And neither has Jason."

My audience just sat there.

I could almost feel the quiet. Then, suddenly, it dawned on me. I hadn't seen January since he took off after butterflies! I looked all around. No dog! Oh, no!

I stood up. "You'll have to babysit each other for a little while," I explained. "B. B., you're in charge. I have to hunt for January."

The trouble was I didn't have any idea where to look. Butterflies can go anywhere!

"January!" I called.

Silence.

Where could he be? I saw a butterfly and started to walk across the meadow. Then I stopped. What I really needed was Help.

14

I closed my eyes. "Please, Lord," I said out loud, "help me find January! He's probably so scared. He can't help it that he's so stupid. Make it so he stays in one place. And, please help me to look wherever he is! Amen."

I had never before explored any farther upstream. From the time I discovered Flat Rock, it became my own special place. I did show it to my father right after school was out. But my only companions all summer have been B. B. and Audrey and Gomer. And, of course, January.

"January," I called again.

Silence.

It seemed a good idea to stay near the stream. If I got lost myself, it would be big trouble!

It's surprising how far you can walk in ten minutes. The stream turned and the path got rocky. And I couldn't even see Flat Rock.

"Jan ... uary! Jan ... uary!"

Silence.

I got careless and slipped. I scraped my knee right through my jeans, but it didn't' bleed.

That's when I remembered Jesus and the lost lamb! In the picture in my Bible, Jesus has the lamb draped over his shoulders.

My family has read Bible stories as long as I can remember. Actually, in the beginning of this story, there started out to be a hundred sheep.

15

But, somehow, one got lost. And Jesus loved that one little lamb so much that He left the others and went in search of the missing one.

I was just about to turn back when I saw him. "January!"

My dog was just lying on his back in the sun! All his legs were waving in the air!

Suddenly, I found myself laughing so hard I was nearly crying. "January, you stupid dog," I said. He rolled over, and I kneeled down and put my arms around him. His nose was cold and wet. And his tail started thumping and couldn't seem to stop.

I guess, to make my story good, I probably should have draped January around my neck. But, frankly, he is too big now, and I wouldn't have been able to take a step.

Instead, January just trotted back beside me. Once he spotted another butterfly, and I smiled as I watched him run ahead.

"Thank you, Jesus," I said, remembering. "Thank you for helping me find my dog. You know, Lord," I said, "I have the feeling January didn't even know he was lost!"

January Plays Watchdog

Just when we were ready to start climbing Flat Rock, January sat down.

"Come on, January," I urged. "Let's pick up the dolls and go back to Dad."

The dumb dog just sat there.

"I don't want to leave you here," I said.

Suddenly, January pointed his nose in the air and began to howl. *AaaOooooo!* He sounded just like he was trying to sing "The Star Spangled Banner"!

All I could do was giggle. The stupid dog just sat there with his nose in the air and kept howling. *AaaOooooo! AaaOooooo!* One soprano howl after another. And I kept giggling.

Well, the last thing in the world I expected to

hear was somebody *else* laughing! But, sure enough, a high, peeling laugh was coming from on top of Flat Rock.

I looked at January with new respect. "Don't tell me you really are a watchdog!" I whispered.

AaaOooooo!

I waited. Frankly, I couldn't think of anything else to do. And, besides, January was still howling. *AaaOooooo!* It may sound like I'm super-brave. Actually, I'm not. Sometimes you have no choice.

AaaOoooooo! AaaOoooooo!

We didn't have to wait long. Almost immediately the owner of the other laugh appeared. She looked kind of like pictures of my grandmother. Except she wore faded jeans, pink jogging shoes, and a backpack.

When January stopped howling and began to growl softly, I felt proud. And, believe it or not, the woman didn't take another step.

She looked at me and smiled. "I couldn't imagine what the owner of that incredible howl might look like!" she said. She glanced at January and started laughing again.

"His name is January," I explained.

"Oh, really?" she laughed. "And wherever did he get a name like that?"

"I named him," I said proudly. "My brother Jason named the last dog."

"I see," she said. "Speaking of names, I'm M. McDuff." She watched January, who had stopped growling. Then she reached out her hand.

I shook it. "I'm Katie Hooper," I said. "What does the M. stand for?"

"I kind of thought you might ask," she said. "It stands for Mayblossom. Mayblossom McDuff."

"And where did you get a name like that?" I asked.

"I was named after a tap dancing teacher."

"Oh," I said. "What shall I call you?"

"Do you think your parents would mind if I let you call me M.?"

"I don't think so," I said. "It's better than May-blossom and certainly a lot shorter."

She laughed again. She looked up toward Flat Rock. "I discovered your friends," she said.

"Please, don't tell anybody," I said. "Most kids my age don't play with dolls anymore."

"But you do," she said. "Any special reason?"

"It's fun. I like to," I confided.

"That's as good a reason as any, I guess." She smiled all the time.

"It can get pretty lonely around here if you haven't got anybody to talk to." I glanced at January. "Of course, I have January, but it's pretty hard to pretend he's anything but a dog."

"I see your point," M. said.

"There aren't any other girls around here. In fact, there aren't any other kids at all," I explained. "Just my brother Jason, and this summer he has a job."

M. nodded.

"Of course, Jason isn't old enough for a real job, but he's helping out at a sheep ranch," I told her. "Do you live around here?"

"I'm on vacation," M. said. "I've always loved the mountains."

"You don't look like a tourist," I observed.

Mary had a little lamb. The sound surprised both of us. We stopped talking.

Mary had a little lamb.

"It's Purple Jeep," I explained. "Well, really it's my father blowing Purple Jeep's horn. I think I'd better go. It was very nice meeting you, M.," I said.

"Same here." M. smiled. "Do you think January will let me past?"

"I think so," I said.

January and I watched M. hike up the creek, where we had just come from.

"Nice lady," I said. "Come on, January! Let's see what Dad wants."

First, we climbed Flat Rock. I didn't say a word to the dolls as I stuffed them into my backpack. So, naturally, they didn't say anything back! As I fastened the buckle, I thought about

Bronco Bob and Gomer: they won't hold it against me that I didn't feel like talking. Audrey I wasn't so sure about! I grinned.

"Sometimes I wish I had some real friends," I told January, as we hiked back toward Purple Jeep. "A fantasy world has its limitations!"

Naturally, January didn't agree or disagree. That was the trouble, I thought. In a make-believe world, no one argues with you. Maybe that's why I get such a kick out of Audrey!

"I hope nothing's wrong," I told January. On other trips up here Dad had paid no attention to time. Whenever I came wandering back was OK with him.

Today we found my father still wearing his hat and pacing back and forth near his easel. "Well, Katie," he said, "what do you think?" He glanced toward his painting.

I walked over and looked. "Oh, Dad!" I exclaimed. "It's beautiful! It's by far the prettiest mountain you've ever done!"

He grinned. "Do you really think so?"

I stood back the way he had showed me. That's how you can stop seeing brush strokes and see the picture as a whole. The colors were gentle, almost pastel. And my father had captured the lighting perfectly! The mountain almost glowed.

I ran over and hugged him. "It's wonderful,

Dad!" I said. "Really, it is!"

"Katie," Dad smiled, "you sound a lot like your mother!" Now I glowed.

We ate our lunch quickly. Afterwards, we piled everything back into Purple Jeep. As we started off, Dad grinned again and blew the horn.

Mary had a little lamb.

In the back seat, January opened one eye, closed it again, and thumped his tail twice. Then he went to sleep.

We rattled and banged along without talking. But just before we turned into our lane, Dad spoke. "If nobody buys it," he said, "I think I'll hang it over the fireplace."

My Mother, the "Duck"

When Purple Jeep rattled to a stop, Mom was shelling peas on a bench in front of the cabin. Smiling, she stood up. "Welcome home," she said.

I'm always surprised when I first see Mom. I guess it's because all my life she's been tall and thin. Now, with the baby due next month, she looks like a light bulb. Or a pregnant duck.

Don't get me wrong. Mom's face is still beautiful! Personally, except for her stomach, I don't think she looks all that different from the snapshots taken at her wedding. They don't have many pictures because she and my father eloped! It must have been very romantic!

"Hi, Mom!" I called. "How are you feeling?"

"Fine, Katie," Mom said, smiling at me. But then she looked at Dad. "How did it go, Darling?"

I turned to watch Dad's face. He was still wearing his hat. But somehow he looks altogether different when he looks at Mom. I can't describe it. But anybody could tell how much he loves her!

"I think it went fine," Dad said. "But I'll let you be the judge." He started to hold up the painting.

"Don't just show me that way," she protested. "Set it up on display. I won't look until you're ready." Mom put her hands over her face like kids do when they're playing hide-and-seek.

Dad slipped right into the game. Grinning at me, he removed the painting and carefully set it on the easel. Still grinning, he tiptoed around the corner of the cabin. For such a heavy man, he sure moves easily. Then he peeked around the corner to watch Mom. "OK, Elizabeth! Ready!" he yelled. Then he whistled a fanfare.

Mom squealed. Slowly, she kind of waddled over to take a good look. At first she didn't say a word. I glanced at Dad. His eyes were sparkling.

"Oh, Steve," she said slowly. "It's wonderful! Really it is!" She stood looking at the canvas.

"Do you really think so?"

"It's beautiful," she smiled. "It's certainly the

25

most beautiful mountain you've ever done!"

By now Dad had come out from his hiding place. He hugged her, kind of from the side.

I watched my parents. They are so special!

But then January woke up and started whining.

"Come on, January," I urged. "It's OK. We're home." But the dog had forgotten how to get out of Purple Jeep. I couldn't believe it! I actually had to help him down!

"I'll be in my room," I told my parents. "Mom, let me know if I can help you."

But neither of my parents said a word.

* * * * * * * *

I left January downstairs when I climbed the ladder to the loft. Frankly, my backpack was about all I could handle. And my stupid dog didn't seem very funny any more.

By the light of day, my room was a disaster. But, as usual, it didn't bother me. The only time it bothers me is when I can't find something.

I looked over at Jason's room. His door was open. His bed was made, and everything was picked up. I can't figure out how come he's so neat. He's so neat, it's almost sickening!

"We're home," I told the dolls. I stuck B. B. and Gomer on the window sill. When I picked up

Audrey, I held her in my hands for a second. Then, impulsively, I closed my arms around her in a big hug. We just stood there.

Finally, I sat on the edge of my bed. "I love you, Audrey," I said.

"I love you, too," said Audrey.

"Audrey," I told her, "don't take this personally, but I'm beginning to wish I had a friend. Even during school, I have to take the bus right home. I never get to play with anyone."

Audrey just smiled her weak little smile.

"I've got an idea!" I said. "I'll pray for a friend." I told her about how the Lord helped me find January. "So, you see, God isn't too busy to help kids!"

For once, Audrey didn't argue.

I closed my eyes. "Please send me a friend, Lord Jesus," I said out loud. I opened my eyes.

Looking at Audrey, I realized I had spoken longer to my doll than I had to Jesus! I closed my eyes again. "Thank you for a wonderful day, Lord," I said. "Did You wake me? I kind of think You might have! Please help Purple Jeep to keep running! Thanks again for helping me find January. Oh, and please encourage somebody to buy Dad's wonderful painting. Amen."

I opened my eyes. Audrey had slipped to the floor. I picked her up, hugged her again, and put her next to my pillow.

* * * * * * * *

Just as I was climbing back down the ladder, I heard Purple Jeep start up and clatter away.

"Can I help you, Mom?" I asked as I came into the kitchen.

She smiled. "Let's finish the peas," she said. "And you can tell me all about your day."

Mom laughed her head off when I told her all the stories about January. "He's the comic relief of the summer!" she said.

"Do you think it's my fault that he's so stupid?" I asked.

"Are you kidding?" she replied. "Of course not! I think the Lord just knew the Hoopers needed something to laugh at!"

"Well, that's a relief!" I giggled.

The peas bonked against the pan.

"Up near Flat Rock, I met an old lady wearing pink jogging shoes," I said.

"Wonderful," Mom replied.

"Really, I did," I explained.

"Did she tell you her name?" Mom asked.

I grinned. "It's Mayblossom McDuff!"

Mom laughed. "How did you think that name up?"

"I didn't make it up," I said. "She was named after a tap dancer!" I giggled.

"Right!" Mom giggled, too.

"She told me I can call her M. for short," I laughed.

"Did you introduce her to B. B.?" Mom asked.

"I didn't have to," I giggled. "They had already met!"

"Katie, Katie," Mom sighed. "You're the most wonderful thing that ever happened to me!"

"Not counting Dad?" I asked.

Mom put down the peas. "Katie, love isn't like that! It isn't like we have just a limited amount of love, and we have to spread it around. Love doesn't subtract! It keeps multiplying!" She put her arm around me.

"I love you, Mom," I said.

"I love you, too," Mom told me. She gave me a big hug.

"Katie, can you help me do some things around here tomorrow morning?"

"Sure," I said. "Will we have time to play a game?"

"Have I ever been too busy?" Mom asked.

"Not so far!" I admitted. "But what about after you have the baby?"

"Is that what this is all about?" Mom asked.

"I don't think so," I said.

Then, just as we finished the peas, Jason rode up on his bicycle. "I'm home!" he yelled.

"And I brought some more wild flowers!"

We Need Money (A Fortune!)

When Mom goes to the hospital to have the baby, I'll be in charge of meals. So I'm learning to cook. Tonight I fried chicken.

"You don't have to turn it so often," Mom said. "Just let it get brown and crusty."

I practiced waiting longer. "How am I doing now?"

"Wonderful!" Mom said. "Just like my mother used to do it!"

"I wish I knew Grandma," I said. "How come she never visits us?"

"It's a long story." Mom didn't say any more, but she wasn't upset. "Let's dish up, Katie. Here's a bowl for the peas."

Dad and Jason, both laughing, jabbed at each

30

other's ribs all the way to the table. Before we sit down to eat, we Hoopers always stand behind our chairs and hold hands while we sing.

"Praise God, from whom all blessings flow; Praise Him, all creatures here below ..." Everyone looked so happy. And I felt wonderful.

"Katie fixed the chicken," Mom announced, as we sat down. She took a wing and passed the platter to my father.

Dad forked a drumstick. "It looks wonderful," he said.

"I just lost my appetite!" Jason teased. I made a face at him, but then couldn't help grinning.

"I washed all the baby clothes today," Mom told us. "Now we're all set except for a crib."

"Would you like to go to the auction Friday night?" Dad asked. "Maybe we could find a baby bed there."

"Maybe we'd better," Mom said. "You never can tell when a baby might surprise you by coming early."

"What will we do if nobody's selling a crib?" Jason asked.

"Think positive," Dad smiled. "Somebody's always getting rid of a baby crib!"

I decided not to tell my family any more about M. McDuff. But I did tell them about January singing "The Star Spangled Banner."

Jason laughed. "What a dog! Katie, did I tell

you we're expecting puppies at the sheep ranch?"

"Lots of excitement ahead!" Dad said. He looked at Mom. "By the way, I ran into Charlie Rogers in the bank. They have extra peaches. They wondered if we'd like to trade for our extra green beans."

"Sounds great!" Mom said. "But if there's a lot of them, I'll need help with the canning."

"Count me in!" I said. Family projects like that are my absolute favorite times!

"I'll do the peeling," Dad offered.

"I told Cochrans I'd help at the ranch all week," Jason said. "I'm busy until Saturday."

"Then Saturday it is!" Mom beamed. "I love getting ready for winter! I'd make a good bird or squirrel."

"You aren't the only one," Jason laughed. "Have you noticed Dad's woodpile?"

Dad looked proud. "I figure we have almost enough wood for two winters," he said. "It's beautiful to see how God provides for us!"

"Let's remember to pray about the doctor bill," Mom said. "I really can't believe how much it costs now to have a baby! It seems like a fortune!"

"Were Jason and I cheaper?" I asked. Everybody laughed. I guess we were.

"Oh, I meant to tell you," Dad said. "While I

was still in the bank, Harry hung my new painting in the lobby."

"Against the stone wall?" Mom asked. "I'll bet it looks nice there."

"Harry thinks it's my best," Dad grinned. "He said it's like a spiritual experience. The early morning light reminds him of the creation story."

"That's beautiful!" Mom said.

I stood up to clear the table. "Are you going out to paint again tomorrow morning?"

"No," Dad said. "I have to put a new muffler on Purple Jeep." He smiled at Mom. "I'll try to have it finished by noon so you can drive it to your doctor's appointment."

"Yes, thanks," Mom said. "I nearly forgot."

"Will you return my library books?" Jason asked. "They're due Friday."

After she agreed, Mom winked at me. "Katie and I have plans for the morning," she said. "Right?"

* * * * * * * *

Dad pushed his dessert dish aside and propped up his Bible. "Well, now, where were we? Katie?"

"Remember when we did Jesus and the lost sheep?" I asked. "Guess what? I acted it out to-

34

day with January, and it worked!"

"Huh?" Jason said. "What are you talking about?"

I explained about January's getting lost near Flat Rock because he was looking for butterflies. Then I told everybody how I found him but that I couldn't carry him back on my shoulders because he was too heavy.

"I don't get your point, Katie," my brother said.

"I guess you had to be there," I told him.

Mom grinned. "You know Katie always finds a way to make the Bible practical," she said.

"But the sheep in the story were supposed to represent *people*," Jason argued. "Not dogs!"

"Never mind, Jason," Dad said. "That's enough."

Tonight Dad read about a woman who lost a coin and had to hunt all over the house for it. I glanced around and decided that her house must have looked a lot like ours. The truth is that Jason is the only neat person in our family!

After the verses, we all took turns praying. I prayed again for a friend. Jason prayed that somebody will be selling a crib at the auction Friday night. Dad prayed that our baby will be healthy. And Mom prayed that the perfect person will see Dad's painting in the bank and buy it.

After supper, Jason and I always do the dishes. This is his week to wash and mine to dry. I think I like washing better because you get finished first.

"It seems like we always have fried chicken when I'm washing," Jason observed. "I hate to do skillets."

"I didn't decide the menu," I explained.

My brother didn't say another word.

After a while, I couldn't stand it. "You're awfully quiet."

"I was just thinking," Jason said.

"Oh. About what?"

He stopped washing. "I was thinking about our prayers for somebody to buy Dad's painting."

"It's really a wonderful painting," I told him. "I guess you didn't get to see it. Maybe sometime you could visit it in the bank."

My brother got a funny look on his face. "Katie, I've been thinking. Why doesn't Dad just get a job?"

I stopped drying. I couldn't believe my ears.

"Don't look so shocked, Katie. That's how most other people pay their bills."

"But Dad's always been a painter," I said. "That's why he and Mom came to Colorado in the first place. He wanted to paint mountains. It's his dream!"

"Lots of people have dreams," Jason said softly.

"Dreams don't pay doctor bills."

"The Lord has always provided everything we've really needed," I reminded him.

"Think about it, Katie," Jason said. "Sure He provides. But the Lord gets a lot of help from Mom! And now, with the new baby and everything, she won't be able to do it any more."

Jason picked up a big stack of plates and put them in the water.

"Hey, I just dried those!" I yelled. "You put our clean dishes back in the dishpan!"

"I'm sorry, Katie," Jason said. "I didn't mean to do it. Really! Give me your towel."

I calmed down. "I'm sorry I hollered. I know you wouldn't do that on purpose."

We stopped talking and concentrated on finishing the dishes. Afterwards, I watched Jason dry his hands and go outside. He didn't even put on a jacket.

* * * * * * * *

Without a word to my parents, I climbed the ladder to my room. I flopped down on my bed.

I couldn't stop thinking about Dad. I felt so sad. I had never once thought of my father doing anything else besides painting. Being a painter was who he was!

Suddenly, I had to smile. In my imagination, I

dressed Dad up so he could get a job working in the bank! In my mind, he stood there grinning, wearing a huge black suit with a red striped tie.

And then I started to giggle. Covering my father's thinning hair I imagined a yellow beret!

Mom's Treasure Hunt

Mom grinned and stacked her breakfast dishes in the sink. "I feel lucky," she said. "Let's set up the game."

I grinned back. I felt pretty lucky myself! "I'll get it."

But when I looked around, I didn't see the backgammon board. I wandered over to the couch and lifted up some newspapers. But all I found was a colored pencil—the missing purple one. "Have you seen the board?" I asked. "I can't seem to find it."

"It can't be too far away," Mom said.

I looked under Dad's sweatshirt. "I found my library book!" I said. I can't believe it. I thought I'd hunted everywhere for it.

Mom stood in the doorway and looked around the room, as if seeing it for the first time. "Katie," she said, "this house is a mess!"

I looked around. She was absolutely right!

"I've got an idea." Mom's eyes twinkled.

"Why do I think it has something to do with cleaning house?" I giggled.

"Are you kidding!" Mom laughed. "You should know by now that I never clean house! This is called a Backgammon Board Hunt!"

I took another look at the room. "Do you think this is the way the person in the Bible story looked for her lost coin?"

"I wouldn't be a bit surprised," Mom giggled. "And we mustn't forget that Colorado is gold mine country. Who knows what treasure lies hidden under an innocent-looking rock!"

She lifted a dusty piece of art board and pulled out a green golf hat. "Not exactly gold, but this is one of your father's favorite hats."

"Did Dad ever play golf?"

Mom looked surprised. "Not since I've known him," she said.

I started with the coffee table. Actually, I couldn't see it, but it had to be under there somewhere. "It's my lucky day!" I held up a valentine. I got it from PeeWee Robinson. I didn't tell Mom he had sent one just like it to every girl in the class.

"How romantic!" Then Mom laughed and held up her latest find. "No wonder Steve couldn't find his clean socks!"

As I caught sight of the coffee table, I started a pile of recovered treasure to take up to my room. So far, I had the library book, the valentine, and my backpack. I couldn't remember how that got back downstairs. I put everything at the bottom of the ladder.

Katie, *that's* what we need in this house!" Mom said.

I turned and looked at her.

Mom pointed to my pile of stuff at the bottom of the ladder. "It's an *As You*," she explained.

"I don't get it."

Mom laughed. "We could put a bench or a box there," she said. "Then you and Jason could take your things up to your rooms *As You* go. We always had an *As You* when I was growing up."

"But Jason never leaves anything around," I pointed out.

"Then it can be yours, Katie," she said. "Some people need an *As You* more than other people."

I grinned. She was right. I added my ball-point pen to the growing pile.

Suddenly, Mom began singing "Joy To The World." She held up the little angel that sits on top of our Christmas tree.

"Let me hold her," I said.

"That's probably why she's still hanging around the house," Mom giggled. "She missed her flight when all the other ornaments took off after the holidays."

"Well, another few moments won't hurt," I said. "I doubt if Dad can find the box of ornaments anyhow."

I smoothed the angel's hair and set her on the coffee table.

"From now on, would you mind conducting your search on the floor?" Mom asked. "Bending over isn't easy, and I'm getting tired."

"Sure." I poked around the piles of stuff next to the couch. "I found some pressed flowers!"

"Are they dry yet?" Mom asked. "Jason brought them up from the meadow when he first started working at the ranch. Remember, we talked about making plaques to sell at the flea market? Maybe we could still do it."

Already the living room looked tidier than it had all summer. And the pile of things headed for my room was getting huge. I wondered how large an *As You* could get.

"What do you know," Mom said. "Here's my recipe for seafood crepes. Maybe I'll try this out next time your father goes trout fishing."

"Speaking of fishing," I said, "here's that lure Dad lost!"

"Oh, no!"

"What's wrong?" I asked.

"I just found two unopened letters addressed to your father. I hope they aren't bills that never got paid!" She walked over and handed me the envelopes. "Just put them out on the coffee table for your father." She stopped and smiled. "Hey, Katie, doesn't it look nice in here?"

"Let's try to keep it this way," I said.

Mom nodded. She already had her nose in a book.

I had to make two trips from the *As You* up to my room. I was clearing a place on my dresser when I spotted the backgammon game. Suddenly, I remembered that Jason and I had played a couple of nights ago. "I found it!" I called to Mom.

Back downstairs, Mom was looking around and smiling. "I love this cabin! This is such a lovely room," she said. "Katie, why don't you bring me that pitcher of wild flowers. Let's try them over here."

And that's how we got started rearranging "accessories." Years ago Mom taught me about accessories—pillows, plants, and things you put around a room to make it cozy and inviting. It is lots of fun to switch everything around to make the room look different. Sometimes we even move the furniture, but not today.

I smiled approval at Mom. The pitcher really

looked nice in its new spot. Of course, that meant we now had to find a new place for the driftwood that used to be there. I tried the driftwood on the mantel. That meant we needed a new spot for the wooden rooster.

Mom and I raced around carrying stuff. And we got happier and happier. Finally, we calmed down and admired our work.

I nodded and smiled. Then I walked over and fluffed up a navy blue pillow and tossed it into the corner of the couch.

Mom swung a small chair around to give it a view from the big window.

I stacked the magazines on the coffee table and lined the books up between two wooden boxes.

Mom even put a plant in the fireplace! She told me she had seen one like that in a magazine.

We never did actually clean anything. But I was as excited as Mom about how nice everything looked.

"Let's keep it this way!" Mom said.

"Absolutely," I agreed.

The "gold rush" had yielded precious treasures for everybody except Jason.

"Jason's so neat! Are you sure he wasn't adopted?" I asked.

"Positive," Mom laughed. "But if I didn't know

better, I'd think you were right!"

She helped me clear a space on the dining room table, and we set up our backgammon game. I got to go first. I rolled a six and a one. I grinned. I had Mom sort of blocked right away.

"You're tough," she said. But then she got double fours and leaped right over my blockade. "How's that?" she laughed.

The game ended up with Mom ahead by only one move. It's more fun when it's close. I hate it when I get trapped!

"Katie, you're really getting good," Mom said.

"When I play with Jason, he always wins."

"He beats me, too," Mom laughed.

"Mom?"

"Yes, Katie?"

"I was wondering. Are we poor?"

"Poor!" Mom laughed. "I can't think of anyone richer! Each of us loves Jesus, and we all love each other! These days, that's pretty special!"

"But how about money?" I asked.

"We've never needed much money," Mom said. "We don't spend a lot. And the Lord always makes sure we have what we need."

"Will things be different after you have the baby?" I asked.

"I don't know what you mean," Mom said. She smiled. "Would you like to ride to town with me this afternoon?"

45

I grinned. "Wonderful!" I said.

Mary had a little lamb. We heard Purple Jeep's horn, and then Dad came in for lunch.

Mom headed for the refrigerator.

I folded up the backgammon game and put it on the coffee table. Right next to the Christmas tree angel ... and the pressed flowers ... and Mom's blue sweater ... and the unopened mail.

January Goes to Town

"Please take January with you," Dad said. "He whined all morning while I was fixing the muffler. I'm afraid I had to promise him he could have a ride."

"Only if Katie will be responsible," Mom said. "Katie?"

"Well, sure," I agreed. Why not? Ever since he was born, January has always loved riding in Purple Jeep. Now he waited in the back seat with his tongue hanging out.

"Can you work out something for supper?" Mom asked Dad. "We may be late."

"I'll not only work out something," Dad said, "I'll work out something special!"

Mom said, "Thanks, Steve."

As we rattled off, Dad stood in the lane and waved. On the smooth highway and with the new muffler, Purple Jeep felt like a sports car. Well, almost.

"In all the years we've lived here, I've never taken Colorado's beauty for granted," Mom said. We were nearly at the divide.

Mom's right. The drive to Woodland Park is beautiful. Now the snow is gone from all but the highest peaks. Dad always says that when he paints a sky this bright blue it doesn't look real. You really do have to be there.

Mom's appointment with the doctor was the first thing on her list. She offered to let me go in with her, but I decided to stay in Purple Jeep with the dog. Once I had gone in. Frankly, I couldn't relate to all those baby magazines. Also, the nurse kept calling me "Big Sister"!

"I have the first afternoon appointment," Mom said. "I don't think I'll have to wait too long."

"I'll be here," I said.

Once the car stopped, January woke up. He put his paws up on the window frame, leaned out, and looked around.

I couldn't believe all the people! This is tourist season, and people from all over the country come to spend their vacations in Colorado. I'm not totally sure why because I've never been anywhere else.

"Look at the funny dog!" A small boy wearing cowboy boots stopped to point at January.

"Don't point, Matthew," his mother said. "It isn't polite."

January opened his mouth and yawned.

"The funny dog is bored," Matthew laughed.

"Come on, Son." Matthew's father dragged him down the street.

I reached around and patted January. "If you ask me, the kid was boring," I said. "Good dog." He thumped his tail so loud I laughed.

Next I started watching all the cameras. Nearly every tourist wears one on a cord around his neck. They kind of bounce along. However, I didn't see a single person taking a picture. I grinned and looked toward the sidewalk where people were walking. Maybe somebody would take a picture of me. But nobody did. I guess they prefer mountains.

I watched a family of five move along from store window to store window. All five were wearing matching shirts. I wondered where they got them.

Next I saw an old couple strolling along eating ice cream cones. I wondered if my grandmother ever eats ice cream cones. This grandma smiled at me. I smiled back. January panted.

Nearly all of the teenage tourists giggled. And they walked the slowest. Even slower than the grandparents. One group walked so slowly they nearly stopped. "Look," giggled a girl with red hair. "It's a purple jeep!"

I giggled, too. It is pretty funny.

The first pregnant person to walk by turned out to be my mother!

"Hi," I said. "That was quick."

"The doctor was in a hurry," Mom said, as she climbed into Purple Jeep. "He was on his way to the hospital to deliver another baby."

It was the first time I stopped to realize that Mom has to share the doctor with other mothers and babies.

"What if two babies decide to be born at the same time?" I asked.

"I don't know," Mom said. "It probably doesn't happen very often."

I realized I had what my Sunday-school teacher calls a *Prayer Opportunity*. "Lord, please give Mom first dibs on the doctor," I said. Nobody but Jesus could tell I was praying because I didn't close my eyes.

"Feel like some ice cream?" Mom asked.

"Sure."

When we parked again, January must have known why. Before we even got out of Purple Jeep, the dog was starting to whine.

"Does he like ice cream cones?" Mom asked.

"Who doesn't?" I said.

"What flavor?"

It depends on what they have." I followed Mom into the small shop.

We ended up with vanilla for Mom, chocolate chip for me, and strawberry for January. Mom and I giggled all the way back out to the car.

"If I hold it for him, do you think he could lick it?" I asked.

"Why don't you try it?" Mom said.

And that's how I got my picture taken after all. A big crowd of tourists stopped to watch January eating an ice cream cone. And a man took our picture. Actually, right afterward, January started showing off. He got greedy and knocked the ice cream off the cone, so he had to jump down and slurp the whole thing into his mouth!

Mom and I couldn't stop laughing. We laughed until we got tears in our eyes. January just curled up for another nap.

"Do you think we can leave January alone?" Mom asked, when she pulled up in front of the yard goods store.

"He's never wandered away yet," I said.

But, frankly, it wasn't much fun in the store. While Mom hunted in the pattern books, I looked at the pictures. But mostly I didn't like the colors.

"They're just pictures," Mom explained.

"When you sew, you can make a dress in whatever fabric you choose."

Finally Mom decided to forget the books and look at the material. I fell in love with some with pink teddy bears on it.

"I think that's meant for pajamas," Mom said.

"Oh," I said. Although I could see her point, all the other material looked very boring.

"I think I'll try again another day," Mom said. "My back is getting tired."

When we got to the library, Mom waited in the car while I went inside. It took a while. I had to wait while a tourist tried to get a library card. She said she would absolutely die if she couldn't read. She didn't care what anybody else thought: this town was the most boring place in the United States!

Finally, I returned Jason's books and mine that I had found in the living room. I had to pay a 19 cent fine. Since I didn't have time to look, I didn't take out any new books.

When I got back to Purple Jeep, both Mom and January were asleep. I slipped into the front seat, but Mom woke up right away. "Oh," she said, "I must have dozed off."

Mom glanced at her watch. "We just have time to stop by the bank. Would you like to see Dad's painting in the lobby?"

"Sure." I couldn't remember seeing one of

Dad's paintings hanging anywhere except at home. Mostly, they are hanging all over our cabin.

January woke up again, so Mom and I decided to take turns going into the bank. I went first.

Dad's newest painting hung all by itself against a stone wall. I've never seen anything so beautiful in my whole life! As I stood there, five other people came and looked. I was so proud. I wanted to tell them that the artist is my father! But then they walked away. So I didn't.

"It's wonderful!" I told Mom. "It looks even more beautiful than it did outdoors."

"I'll be right back," Mom said. She struggled awkwardly out of Purple Jeep. I wonder if she'll ever walk like a normal person again.

Suddenly, as I waited, January started to howl. *AaaOoooooo!* It was his "Star Spangled Banner" routine. I turned around to try to make him stop, but he wouldn't. His nose was in the air, and he just kept howling. *AaaOooooo! AaaOoooooo!* Finally, I turned back and decided to pretend I didn't notice him.

Then I saw her! There, on the sidewalk walking away from the bank, was M. McDuff! It couldn't have been anyone else. She even had on the same pink jogging shoes.

"What's the matter?" I asked January. "Don't you like her?"

AaaOoooooo! AaaOoooooo! January kept howling until M. was out of sight.

And that's when Mom came back out to the car. "Katie, you're absolutely right!" she said. "The painting is even more beautiful hanging against that stone wall!"

Dad's Treasure Hunt

"I saw her!" I told Mom.

"Who?"

"M.," I said. "M. McDuff. The person I met at Flat Rock."

"Katie," Mom asked, "is M. a real person?"

"Of course," I told her. "What do you think she's doing here?"

Mom didn't answer. How could she? She didn't believe M. really existed!

"Let's put on our sweaters," Mom said. "It will be chilly by the time we get home." She started the motor and Purple Jeep lurched forward.

Well, for some reason I couldn't get M. off my mind. Was it really M. McDuff? How could I be so sure? I had only talked to her for a few minutes. And Flat Rock is on the other side of the divide—miles from here.

Suddenly, January whined.

"That's it," I told Mom. "January recognized her, too! And January never pretends!"

"I'm sorry I doubted you, Katie," Mom said. "You've spent your entire life talking to fantasy characters. And they always seem so real to you!"

I could see her point. "I do know the difference," I said. "And Mayblossom McDuff is real!"

"So tell me about her," Mom said.

Well, there wasn't very much to tell. "She looks kind of like a grandmother," I explained. "She has short, gray hair. Yesterday she was wearing a backpack. Her jeans are old—not stiff like the ones most tourists wear. And she wears pink jogging shoes."

I glanced at Mom. She never took her eyes off the road, but I knew she was listening.

"M. is the kind of person who really likes kids," I continued. "Not all adults do, you know. A lot of people just fake it."

"And you liked her?" Mom asked.

"Oh, yes. She was like an old friend. And she has the most incredible laugh."

"Well, maybe we'll see her again," Mom said. "I'd like to meet her."

There was still one problem, but I decided not

to mention it. January's howling. He's never acted that way with anybody else in his whole hilarious life.

When we got home, Jason was waiting outside the cabin. "What's going on?" he asked.

"Is something going on?" Mom said as she and I climbed down from Purple Jeep.

"I just got home," Jason said. "I didn't see anybody around, and the cabin's locked."

"Did you look in the secret place?" I asked. My brother shook his head. I ran over and lifted the mat. I pulled out a piece of paper clipped to several envelopes.

It was one of Dad's pencil drawings. He had sketched what looked like a treasure chest. Spilling out of the top were items of food—pie, cake, a turkey, sandwiches, bananas, apples, a loaf of bread, a pork chop, an egg, and even a jar of sweet pickles.

I grinned. "It's a treasure hunt!"

"It looks like we have to hunt for our supper," Mom said.

Clipped to the back of the drawing were three envelopes. I unclipped them. Sure enough, each one was identified by a symbol.

One of the things that's fun about being a Hooper is that you get your own symbol. Every person in the family has one. Dad's symbol is a tree. Mom's is a lamb. Jason's is a rainbow. And, probably because I was born on Valentine's Day, my symbol is a heart.

I handed the envelope with the *lamb* on the front to Mom, who held it and waited. "Here's yours," I told Jason. Naturally, I kept the *heart* for myself.

"We haven't had a treasure hunt all summer," I said. "I nearly forgot about them."

"OK," Mom said. "Let's begin."

We all started tearing open our envelopes to find our first clues. They would show us where to look for the next ones.

What I found inside was a sketch of a bird feeder with a tiny bird sitting on it. Since we have only one feeder, I headed for the back of the cabin.

But I couldn't find my second clue. Finally, I saw something white sticking out of the sunflower seeds in the feeder! Sure enough! I pulled out another envelope with my heart symbol on it.

My second sketch showed three little trees with an arrow under the middle one. It was too easy! I ran to the trees in front of our cabin. Wrong! No clue! Then I started to giggle. I realized they weren't big trees after all!

I ran all the way to the field where we had planted hundreds of tiny pine seedlings. At first, I thought finding an envelope there would be hopeless! But then I saw the arrow stuck into the second row. Attached to the shaft was my next clue!

I sat down to open the envelope. Glancing back at the cabin, I saw Jason climbing on the roof! And Mom was sitting on the bench next to the front door. She waved to me, and I waved back.

My clue showed a bedroom filled with clutter—clearly belonging to me! Audrey was even there! An arrow pointed under my bed. Now I had a problem: How could I get up to my room? Maybe that was why Jason was climbing on the roof.

I ran back to the cabin. "What's wrong, Mom," I said. "Did you give up?"

"Are you kidding?" Mom grinned. "No, my last clue instructed me to sit here and wait for you and Jason before I opened the door."

Just then, Jason climbed down. "My next clue is in the fireplace," he said. He showed us his drawing.

Mom showed us hers. "Mine is in the bathtub," she laughed. "Let's try the door."

This time when Jason turned the knob, the door swung open.

Inside, Dad was sitting at the table laughing at us. "Hurry up," he urged. "I'm hungry!"

I watched Jason head for the fireplace. "All

right!" he said. He lifted out our bean pot. I could smell the baked beans. I can't remember anything ever smelling so good!

Mom returned from the bathroom with a plate full of oatmeal cookies.

"Come on, Katie," Dad said. "We still need your contribution."

"If it's in her room, we're in big trouble," Jason laughed. "We could all starve before she finds it!"

While my family waited, I climbed the ladder and went into my room. I lifted the edge of a blanket which hung onto the floor. I looked under the bed. I couldn't see anything. When I squatted down and reached under, I felt something. It was a bed I had made for Audrey. I also pulled out a notebook, some red yarn, and a hundred dollar bill from the Monopoly game! Finally, I discovered a basket filled with apples.

Dad came over and stood under the ladder. "Do you need help?" he asked. "Don't drop it."

We took our places around the table and sang "Praise God, from whom all blessings flow ..." Already on the table were rolls and butter and glasses of milk.

"What fun!" Mom said.

"I couldn't believe I had a clue up on the roof!" Jason exclaimed.

Dad looked pleased. "I told you I'd fix something special for supper," Dad told Mom, as he helped her into her chair.

"Hey, everybody, please save your sketches for my collection," I said. Jason reached into his pocket and handed me his clues. Mom said hers were on the coffee table.

"The cabin sure looks beautiful," Dad said. Mom and I grinned.

"I'll be happy to vacuum after we finish the dishes," Jason offered. "I don't get many chances when the floor is this empty!"

I told Dad we had stopped by the bank. "Lots of people were standing in the lobby looking at your painting," I said. "I felt so proud."

"I feel like I missed out," Jason said. He smiled at Dad. "I wish you had kept your painting here until I could have seen it. I'll stop by the bank the next time I get library books."

"You should hurry," Mom said. "This one is so good, it probably won't be hanging there long!"

Although the cookies Dad baked were kind of hard, everybody praised them anyway. And while we ate our apples, I told everybody the latest story about January eating a strawberry ice cream cone. Everybody laughed.

Just before Dad read our Bible passage, Mom remembered something. "In case I forget, Steve," she said, "there's some old mail on the coffee table."

"I'll check it when we're finished," he said.

While the rest of us listened, Dad read the Bible story about the lost son.

But when my father got to the part when the younger son was eating with pigs, my mind wandered. I tried to picture Jason eating with pigs. Yuck! He was oozing with mud from head to toe!

Dad gave me a stern look. "It isn't funny, Katie," he said.

Well, the only way I could think of to get my brother clean again was to turn a hose on him! But then, in my imagination, Jason started hollering. The water was like ice! The mud-covered Jason was racing all around trying to get away!

There was no way I could stop laughing. I got hysterical. It was catching, and in no time our whole family was laughing. And none of them even knew why!

"OK," Dad said, finally, wiping a tear from his eye, "I give up. We'll just take it from there tomorrow night."

A Surprise from Denver

Jason and I were still doing the dishes when Dad called us into the living room. "Please sit down," he said. "I have something to read to you." He looked very serious.

Still feeling giggly, I sat on the floor and tucked my feet under me. Jason flopped down on the blue chair. Mom was already sitting next to Dad on the couch.

"I'd like you to hear this letter," Dad told us. "It's from a bank in Denver." He read slowly.

Dear Mr. Hooper:

This is to let you know that Jeffrey Allen, the owner of your rental property, has written to us

*from California asking that we put the cabin and
fifty acres up for sale.*

*As you no doubt realize, Mr. Hooper, property
values have risen dramatically in the fifteen
years since he moved from Colorado. The Allens
have separated, and Mr. Allen no longer has
plans to return from California. He has been ad-
vised that his rental income is too low for his
capital investment.*

*Since you have been renting the cabin for so
long, Mr. Allen has asked our firm to give you the
first opportunity to buy it. If you are interested,
Mr. Hooper, please telephone our office for further
details.*

> *Sincerely,*
> *Arthur Bennington,*
> *Agent*

Nobody said a word. This cabin has always
been our home. I can't even imagine living anywhere else.

"I used to wonder how Jeff was doing," Dad
said. "But for a long time now I've just sent the
rent off to his agent every month."

"You know the owner?" Jason asked.

"Yes," Mom said. "Jeff and Linda Allen were
part of the original group of friends who came
here from Illinois."

65

"When Linda's father died, they invested her inheritance in this piece of land," Dad told us. "But they had hardly moved into the cabin when Jeff decided that the best place to make money was California."

"They always planned to come back to Colorado," Mom told us. "They needed somebody to take care of their cabin while they were gone, so they rented it to us."

"It worked out perfectly for us," Dad said. "Your mom and I loved this land. And we were hoping that the Lord would give us a family."

Mom smiled at Jason. "You were born the following year."

"I guess buying the cabin will cost a lot of money," I said.

Jason laughed nervously. "There's probably no point in asking, is there?" He looked at Dad.

"With the Lord, nothing is impossible," Dad said. "If He wants us to keep living here, He'll make a way. But He doesn't have much time. The letter was sent two weeks ago!"

"Oh, my," Mom said. "I think we should talk to the Lord." She closed her eyes. Before I could even close mine, she was praying: "Lord, You are so good to us! For fifteen years You've provided our family with a wonderful home here in this beautiful country. Lord, how we thank You!"

"Father, we've always loved it here," Dad prayed. "It's the only home the children know. If it's Your will, please show us how we can stay."

I took a deep breath. "Lord, You own the cattle on a thousand hills," I prayed. "So this probably isn't even a big deal to You."

"Lord, I'm asking You for the money we'll need to buy the property," Jason prayed. "The land really belongs to You, Lord. We promise we'll take good care of it."

The room was quiet, so Dad said, "Amen." Then he told us he'd call the agent in Denver tomorrow morning.

Jason and I went back to the dishes.

"I love this cabin," I said.

"I don't even want to talk about it," Jason said. We finished the dishes in silence.

When we were finished, Dad had an idea. "Hey, everybody, it's a beautiful evening. Let's take a walk."

"If you don't mind, I'll stay here and do the vacuuming," Jason said. Dad didn't mind. My brother plugged in the old machine and started cleaning behind the couch. I've never seen him move so slowly.

Mom, Dad, and I put sweatshirts on. When we got to the door, I turned. "Come on, January," I called. Nothing happened.

I looked at Mom. "I don't think I've seen the

dog since we got home. Have you?" She shook her head.

Dad gave his shrill whistle. It was even louder than the vacuum cleaner. Still no sign of January. I hated to leave without him, but I had no choice.

We walked slowly toward the west. Before our very eyes, the big, red ball of a sun dropped down and then disappeared.

"Remember our first winter in the cabin?" Dad asked.

"I'll never forget it," Mom laughed. "All our friends were north of Denver—many miles away. And we had no car. I decided if we made it through that first winter, we could live through anything!"

"Remember how it kept snowing?" Dad asked. "And we couldn't even afford to rent skis! More than once, I was tempted to wonder if your parents were right."

"Don't talk that way," Mom laughed. "You know I never would have let you go to Colorado and leave me behind."

"Didn't Mom's parents like you?" I asked my father.

"Oh, they liked me, I guess. I don't think it was anything personal," Dad said. "But they sure didn't like the idea of their baby going off to Colorado with a painter."

"I was hardly a baby," Mom said. "I was twenty-one years old, and I had graduated from college." She took Dad's hand.

"Mom's older brothers were so practical," Dad said. "Engineering. Business Administration."

"God leads each of us a different way," Mom said. "They had their dream, and we had ours. And Jesus is Lord—even when He sends surprises."

"Especially when He sends surprises," Dad grinned. "Right, Katie?"

"I guess so," I answered.

When we got back, the cabin was nearly dark. Jason was in the living room picking chords on his guitar. And January was sleeping at his feet.

"Where was the dog?" Dad asked.

"Where else? Under the couch," Jason said. "He was shaking like a leaf. It took me fifteen minutes to figure it out. I think he's afraid of the vacuum cleaner!"

"No kidding!" I said.

Jason laughed. "I'll bet this is the first time January's ever seen or heard a vacuum cleaner!"

"Jason!" Mom laughed. "Well, you could be right."

My brother hit a chord and began to sing "His Name Is Wonderful." The rest of us plopped down and joined in. It's the first time we've had a family sing-along since Jason started teaching himself to play. We sounded pretty good.

I took a deep breath. In the dark, our cabin felt so relaxed and cozy and peaceful. We sang every chorus we could think of.

But then January started moaning, and that broke the mood. Dad couldn't stand it. He got up and turned on the light.

"Well, it must be just about bedtime anyway," Mom said. Which sounded like a clue for Jason and me to go up to our rooms. To be honest, it wasn't really very late!

I looked at my brother and he looked at me. After I kissed Dad and Mom goodnight, I followed Jason up the ladder.

Nobody can say we can't take a hint!

I Hunt Some More

When I woke up this morning, I felt different.
I felt like I was going to have an adventure. But
then I couldn't find my underwear.

I rummaged around through the piles of stuff
on my dresser, and on my chair, and on my desk,
and on the floor. No underwear. It probably was
there, but I sure couldn't see it.

Still in my pajamas, I stood in my doorway
and took a good look at my room. Frankly, it
looked like a pig pen!

Although I've heard of kids who get grounded
for not cleaning their rooms, it has never happened to me. For one thing, Mom never comes
up to the loft. And even if she did, she's not the
kind that stresses tidiness.

"Being kind and loving is more important," Mom always says. What Hoopers get grounded for are things like telling a lie, or gossiping about somebody, or not sharing.

Well, I decided to eat breakfast in my robe and hunt later. I'm not sure why, but I pulled my door closed behind me. Maybe because I saw Jason's room—bed made, and as neat as ever. He must have gotten up early.

When I got downstairs, January greeted me. He was so glad to see me, he chased his tail in a circle.

"That's good," I whispered. "Who taught you that trick?"

January stopped chasing and started whining.

"Be still," I whispered, as I poured myself a bowl of cereal. Mom's door was still closed.

I miss having breakfast with Mom. She always used to be in the kitchen when I came downstairs. But now she doesn't sleep well. It has something to do with having a baby.

Propped up in the middle of the table was a note Dad had left for Mom. It was written on a paper towel with a magic marker. It said:

Darling! I'm painting mountains.
        Love forever,
                Steve
P.S. I'll be back for lunch.

Reading it made me feel so good that I smiled.

While I was eating, I decided to do something I hadn't done in ages—clean my room. Hopefully, in the process, I'd find my underwear. And then I could proceed with today's adventure.

I had already made my decision when Mom opened her door. "Hi, Katie," she said. "How are you this beautiful morning?" She wandered over, gave me a kiss, and poured herself a bowl of cereal.

"I lost my clean underwear," I told her.

"That's too bad."

"Don't faint," I said. "But I'm going to clean my room."

She didn't faint. She just said, "That's nice." She was smiling as she read Dad's note.

Back upstairs, I hardly knew where to begin. I decided to start with hanging up clothes. Next, I'd pick up everything on the floor. Then I'd tackle what was left on the furniture.

My dolls weren't much help. Bronco Bob and Gomer watched from the windowsill. Well, B. B. did. Gomer always has a hard time concentrating.

As for Audrey, she was her usual negative self. I kept hearing her voice: "You'll be stuck up here all day," she said.

"No, I won't."

"Ha!"

"Be still, Audrey," I told her. "Just think how nice it's going to look in here!"

Audrey said she couldn't care less, but I thought she'd change her tune when I was finished and my room looked like a picture in a magazine.

The trouble was, I kept finding things that were interesting. Like my experiment with photosynthesis. I really am sorry I killed Mom's plant. But I still think it would have died anyway.

Most of the things in my room are in there because I want to save them. I spent ten minutes looking at my agate collection before I moved it into my bookcase.

Even though it usually looks like a bomb hit it, my room is special. One good thing about a log cabin is that you can stick tacks into the walls. So my room is like a big bulletin board.

Of everything I own, my favorite thing is my collection of Dad's pencil sketches. I especially like the ones he does for me every year for my birthday. I have them all hung in a row above my bed.

Actually, the very first sketch of Katie Hooper was drawn when I was a new-born baby. It shows a bright-eyed little baby with no hair. Framing the sketch is the shape of a heart.

I looked down the row of sketches. It's funny,

but when I look in the bathroom mirror, I never can see myself changing. But the smiling Katie Hooper in the sketches on my wall is growing up!

Suddenly, I thought about our new baby. For the first time, I could imagine her crying. Would Dad draw her picture? Or would it be a boy? That was when I realized that our new baby would need a name. And a Hooper symbol.

I picked up my Superman cape, which I am planning to recycle as as theater curtain for a puppet show. And right there, underneath the cape, was my clean underwear! I started to get dressed. I could finish my room another day.

"Hi, Valentine!" Dad had just come home. He plucked me off the ladder and hugged me.

"Did you paint another masterpiece?" I asked.

"I'm afraid not," he said. "Maybe I need you along to help inspire me."

"I was wondering," I said. "Are you planning to draw sketches of the new baby?"

"Hmmm," Dad said. "I hadn't thought much about it. I suppose I will."

Mom carried in a stack of blankets. "I have everything ready for the crib," she said.

"Tonight's the auction," Dad remembered. "Let's eat early. Right now, I'm going to call Mr. Bennington in Denver."

I decided my adventure could wait a little

longer. I'd hang around and listen while Dad talked. Mom was doing the same thing.

"Hello, Mr. Bennington? This is Steve Hooper," he said. "I'm calling about your letter."

It wasn't much of a conversation, at least not on this end. All Dad did was nod and say, "I see." He sounded like somebody else.

"Yes, we'll be here," he said. "Thank you very much."

He hung up the phone, carried a cup of coffee from the kitchen, and sat down on the couch.

"Well?" Mom asked.

"To be honest, it looks like a closed door," Dad told her. "The good news is that they'll let us buy the property for $25,000 less than the regular price. The bad news is that the price is astronomical." He whispered an amount. "My mind can't even comprehend that much money!"

"You said it would take a miracle," Mom said.

Dad sipped his coffee. "Well, I was right."

"Maybe nobody else will buy it," Mom suggested. "Then we might still be able to stay here."

"Perhaps." Dad looked sad. "But Mr. Bennington already has two prospective buyers who want to see the cabin tomorrow."

"Oh," Mom sighed.

"There's more," Dad continued softly. We waited while he took a deep breath. "One of the buyers wants to put up condominiums!"

"Oh, no," I cried.

At first, nobody else said a word. And at lunch Mom and Dad talked about other things.

After I finished eating, I climbed back up the ladder. I decided I might as well keep plugging away at cleaning my room. Somehow, I had stopped feeling that today was going to bring me some wonderful adventure.

Friday Night Auction

"Praise God, from whom all blessings flow; Praise Him, all creatures here below; Praise Him above, ye heavenly host; Praise Father, Son, and Holy Ghost! Amen."

With Dad's unwavering lead, our mealtime song was as strong as ever. As soon as we sat down at the table, Dad told Jason what Mr. Bennington had said.

My brother listened carefully. "Dad," he said, "I had a lot of time to think today. I decided that if it will help save the cabin, you can have my savings." He reached into his pocket and pulled out his bank book.

I was stunned. As long as I've known him, my brother has been saving every penny!

79

"Jason!" Mom said. "It's your money for college. It's your dream."

"College is still a long way off," Jason said. "And I love this land, too. I thought our family would live here forever!"

At first, Dad had tears in his eyes. He couldn't say a word. Then he reached over and clasped Jason's hand.

"Son, thank you! I feel as if I'm rich in much more than money," he said. "You'll never know what it means to me to feel your unselfish support!" By now, Dad was smiling.

"Compared to the price, I guess it isn't much," Jason said. "But it's a start. Could we borrow the rest of the money?"

"I doubt it," Dad explained. "Banks like to lend money to people who don't really need it."

"Steve," Mom said slowly, "maybe I could ask my mother for a loan."

Dad shook his head. "You know how I feel about that," he said. "No, we'll do like we've always done. We will trust in the Lord. We'll wait for Him."

During our Bible time, Dad had us look up Matthew 6:31 to 34. I got to read it out loud.

So do not worry, saying, "What shall we eat?" or "What shall we drink?" or "What shall we wear?" For the pagans run after all these things, and your heavenly Father knows that you need them. But seek first his kingdom and his righteousness, and all these things will be given to you as well. Therefore do not worry about tomorrow, for tomorrow will worry about itself. Each day has enough trouble of its own.

Dad reminded us that what we need today is a crib! Later, during our prayer time, Dad also prayed again for God's will about the land.

After prayers, we stacked our dishes in the sink and climbed into Purple Jeep. Everybody except January. This time, the dog had to stay at home. All the way out to the road, we could hear him protesting.

We sang all the way to town. Without Jason's guitar, we didn't sound as good as last night. But it sure seemed like we got to the Auction Barn fast!

"'Evening, Elizabeth," said Mr. Darling, who greets everybody at the side door.

"Hi, Clarence." Mom smiled.

"Haven't seen you for a long time," Mr. Darling continued. "We've missed you at the antique auction."

"Thank you," Mom said.

"Any baby things for sale this week?" Dad asked.

"Try looking against the far wall on the left," Clarence said. He and his helpers spend all week setting up the merchandise as it's brought into the barn.

"Hey, I see somebody I know," Jason said. He looked at Dad.

"Go ahead and join your friends, Jason," Dad said. "We'll see you later." My brother hurried off through the crowd.

Tonight there were so many people it was hard for us to stick together. Although the sales don't start that early, the Auction Barn opens at 5 o'clock. We dodged some people who were still eating hot dogs. Whenever we go, the Hoopers always eat at home first.

"Hi, Sara," Mom said. "Hi, Rudy." Mom knows a lot of people. That's because sometimes she sells antiques. Actually, antiques are sold at a separate auction once a month, but some of the same buyers and sellers are involved.

"Now I know I'm ready for the baby," Mom told Dad. She laughed. "In another few weeks, I don't think I'll fit through the aisle!" I was walking behind her, and I think she's right!

"I don't see any baby furniture," Dad said. "Do you?"

Mom and I looked up and down the tables.

"Maybe Clarence meant these clothes," Mom said. She held up a pink terry suit with a zipper

82

up the front and a yellow stain near the collar. "Isn't this cute?"

Behind us, we could hear one of the auctioneers starting to take bids from a group of people clustered around a refrigerator.

"We'd better split up and start hunting," Dad said. "There's got to be a crib here somewhere. Will you be OK by yourself, Katie?"

"Sure," I said. "I'm small. I can scoot in and out fast. Will we meet in the usual place next to the refreshment stand?"

"Right," Mom said. "In about half an hour."

I threaded in and out of the aisles. When I didn't see a crib, I decided to go back into the first room.

"Hi, Katie! Want some of my popcorn?" It was Jenny, a girl in another class at my school.

"Sure," I said. I reached in the bag and pulled out a buttery handful. "Have you had a nice summer?"

"Kind of," she said. "Well, the truth is that Dad's been assigned to a new post, so we have to move again. That's the army for you."

"You move a lot?" I asked.

"Are you kidding? Would you believe I've gone to six schools already?"

"Wow!" I said.

"Mom can't wait to leave," Jenny said. "She's stuck with the move. My father's already stationed in Texas. Tonight we're selling off whatever we could load in our van. Once it's sold, we're gone!"

"Hey," I said, "do I see a baby bed?"

"It's all our baby stuff," Jenny told me. "Mom says no more babies for her. She's not going to move this stuff one more time." She looked around. "Right, Mom?"

Her mother did look tired. As she stood there next to her belongings, she had a strong grip on a small, squirming boy. And another boy was climbing under the tables.

"What am I bid for this beautiful crib?" The auctioneer was trying to get something going. "Who'll give me fifty?"

Nobody said anything. I looked around for Mom and Dad, but they must have still been in the other room. More and more people were gathering around.

"Who'll give me twenty-five?"

Nobody said a word.

"Do I hear ten dollars? Come on, folks," he pleaded.

Suddenly I heard a woman call, "I'll give you ten." She looked like a grandmother.

"I hear ten. Who'll make it twenty?" The caller looked at all the people circling around.

"Twenty!" I heard myself yell.

The caller smiled. "That's the way, folks. She'll

84

show you how to do it! Do I hear twenty-five?"

Twenty-five!" called a man. I couldn't believe it.

"Now, who'll make it thirty?"

No response. The caller looked at me.

I don't know how I knew it, but I did. This crib was meant for a Hooper! It wasn't all beat up like a lot of them are. It was clean and painted gray. And the mattress was pink with little lambs running around all over it.

"Thirty!" I yelled.

"Going once, going twice, and sold to the girl in the blue dress." The man reached down and handed me a ticket. "Congratulations," he said.

"Need a playpen or a highchair?" asked Jenny's mother.

"No thank you." I smiled weakly. And that's when I got scared. I mean, I didn't have a cent! And I had no idea if Mom would think the crib was worth thirty dollars. In fact, suddenly I wondered if she would want it at all!

By the time I reached the refreshment stand, I felt almost sick.

"There you are, Katie," Mom said. "We were wondering where you were!"

I didn't know what to say.

"Katie, see if you can find Jason," Dad said. "There's no crib for sale here tonight. We'll have to come back and try again next week."

"I bought one," I said. "I bought a crib! I hope it's OK." I told my parents what happened. "I didn't have a chance to go and find you."

Well, I've never seen Dad more surprised or Mom more excited. When she saw it, she said the crib was wonderful! Even better than new! And they said the Lord helped me get a great bargain besides!

After Dad paid for it, Clarence helped Dad tie the crib onto the back of Purple Jeep. "That woman brought in a load of stuff at the last minute," he told us. "She said she needed to get rid of it tonight!"

"Katie, see if you can find Jason," Dad said. "Let's celebrate with some ice cream!"

I hadn't seen my brother all evening, and I couldn't see him now, either. Then, just as I was about to give up, I caught sight of him.

Jason was off to one side of the barn leaning against a washing machine. And, in a circle around him, were *six* smiling girls!

Suddenly, for some reason I knew my brother wouldn't be thrilled to see me. Even if it involved an ice cream cone! I turned and walked back to my parents.

Our Canning Is Interrupted

On Saturday mornings, we Hoopers always have pancakes. What woke me up on this particular morning was the smell of bacon. It works even better than an alarm clock!

Today I dressed quickly. Audrey and Gomer were still sleeping, and I didn't disturb them. On the way out I winked at Bronco Bob. B. B. always looks ready for adventure. But he might not be so great at canning peaches.

When I entered the kitchen, Dad greeted me with a big hug. "Katie! We were just about to call you!"

Jason Hooper, assistant cook, was just finishing setting the table. "All we need now is Mom," he said.

"I'll get her," Dad volunteered.

Whenever Dad cooks, he wears this huge apron. Mom made it. It is red striped and has a pocket and very long ties. Regular ties don't reach around him.

Anyhow, Dad wore his apron while he went into the bedroom. We could hear him say something and we could hear Mom giggle.

I turned to Jason. "When I saw your door closed, I thought you might still be in bed."

"You know I always help Dad make the pancakes," my brother said. Although he likes to cook, he wouldn't be caught dead wearing an apron.

I looked at him more closely. Jason looked just exactly the same as he always does. I can't see why those girls would think he's special. "Jason," I said, "who were those girls you were talking to last night?"

He just stood there and grinned. And I knew he wasn't going to tell me anything.

"Well," I said, changing the subject, "is that a great crib, or what! I knew the Lord would answer our prayer!"

"It sounds like we came pretty close to missing it altogether," Jason said.

"But we got it," I said. "Right?"

Mom must have dressed fast. "How come the bacon?" she asked.

"It's a special treat," Dad grinned. "We're having potato pancakes!"

"With applesauce?" I asked.

"My favorite," Mom smiled.

When we were totally stuffed, Mom went into her weekly ritual. First she hugged Dad and Jason and thanked them for breakfast. Then she said what she says every single week. "I sure feel sorry for people who have to eat their pancakes in a restaurant!"

Dad and Jason beamed. Like they always do.

Before we could start canning peaches, we had to wash dishes. Stacking them in the sink only works for so long! Then you run out of something like spoons. Mostly what we were out of this morning was room for all of us to work.

While Mom and I did the dishes, we also washed out our canning jars. Meanwhile, Dad filled the big pot with water and put it on the stove to boil. And Jason carried in the baskets of peaches.

Actually, canning peaches is pretty easy!

The juice just starts out as syrup made from plain sugar and water. You don't even have to cook it. Mom measured the sugar and water into another large pan, and I helped stir it.

Dad and Jason washed off the fruit and started peeling. Then they cut each peach in half and took out the stone.

"Save the pits in this bowl," I pleaded. "I plan to make something out of them." I'm not sure what, but I'll think of something.

Mom showed me how to put the raw peach halves into the clean jars. The rounded part of the peach goes next to the glass. "Here, Katie, you try one."

If you're too slow, the peaches turn brown. I was pretty slow at first. But Mom didn't care. She was filling another jar at the same time.

After the peaches were arranged in the jars, we poured syrup over them. Then we poked around the side of each jar with a knife so the bubbles could float out.

"I'll put on lids," Dad offered.

"Don't screw them too tight!" Mom reminded him. It is part of our Hooper family folklore that one year Dad fastened on jar lids so tight nobody could open them! We had no tomatoes that year!

When Mom and I had eight jars filled, Jason put them into a rack and lowered them into the pan of boiling water. He always gives the jars their hot water bath. Jason is good at timing things.

People in Colorado have to boil things longer than other people do. That's because our altitude is higher. Afterwards, Jason lifts the rack and puts the jars on the table.

"Ping!" One by one, the jar seals snap tight all

by themselves. They make a little *ping* noise. You can always tell a lid that isn't sealed because when you touch it, it wiggles in and out.

Canning is a great family chore. With all the Hoopers helping, we can do all the canning steps at once. It's so much fun seeing our counter fill up with jars.

And, of course, all the time we're working together, we can talk about things.

"If we get finished with the peaches in time, maybe we can set up the crib this afternoon," Mom said.

"Where will you put it?" I asked.

"In the bedroom with Dad and me. That's where you and Jason both started out."

"I can remember when Katie was born," Jason said. "I hated being all alone upstairs. I felt jealous because she got to be in your room."

"Really, Jason? I didn't know that," I said. "I thought I always slept in my room upstairs." But everybody shook their heads.

* * * * * * * *

We had our second batch of peaches in the boiling water when there was a knock at the door.

"I'll get it," Dad said. The rest of us kept working. But we worked slowly and listened.

93

"Steve Hooper? I'm Arthur Bennington. This is Ms. April Morganstern. We've come to see the cabin."

"Would you like me to show you around?" Dad asked.

"It won't be necessary. Go ahead with what you're doing."

Mr. Bennington must have guessed that Dad was cooking, since he was still wearing his red and white striped apron.

Dad brought the visitors back to the kitchen doorway. "This is my family," he said.

We looked up to see a white-haired man. And with him, a beautiful, thin woman. Her blond hair was cut short like a boy's. And her jeans were so tight I wondered how she could walk.

The woman smiled at us. "Charming," she exclaimed. "Just like pioneer days."

Dad didn't reply. He took three long steps to the kitchen table and picked up his paring knife. "Let us know if you have questions," he said.

It was hard to concentrate on just canning peaches. I could hear footsteps upstairs in my room. And then we all heard January starting to whine.

I slid a peach half into my jar. It landed wrong-side out.

January's whining was getting louder. Now

we could hear Mr. Bennington and Ms. Morganstern talking softly in the living room. Then they were back in the kitchen.

While Ms. Morganstern looked around the kitchen, January was really embarrassing. He whined and nuzzled against her leg. He looked up at her like a lovesick puppy.

She patted him. "Does the dog go with the cabin?" she asked.

I couldn't believe it! But before I could protest, Dad said, "She's only kidding." I wasn't so sure.

And January kept whining and nuzzling. When Ms. Morganstern reached down and patted him again, he whined even louder.

They turned to go. "Thank you, Steve," Mr. Bennington said. "I'll be back again later."

We could hear them talk as they left. "You're right, Art. It is charming," said Ms. Morganstern. "It's just too bad the cabin is located where it is. I think this is where the road to the fourth unit would have to go."

I was surprised. Ms. April Morganstern sure didn't look to me like a condominium builder!

Jason had to practically hold January down to keep the dog from trying to jump in the car with her!

"I've never seen January act so stupid," I said. "Why do you think he did that?"

"Maybe he just likes her," Mom answered.

"She *is* a cool lady," Jason said. "But, to be honest, I hope her car gets stuck in a low place in the road!"

"Jason!" Dad said. But then he laughed.

Once the car was gone, Dad told Jason to put January outside. "He probably needs some exercise," Dad said.

We worked without talking much. I wondered when Mr. Bennington would come back.

"Is anyone hungry?" Mom asked. We all shook our heads. Which is why we didn't have lunch.

By the time our counter was filled with jars of peaches, Mom was sitting down at the table. "I've had it," she said.

"Why don't you take a nap?" Dad suggested. "We're almost finished here. We can take care of the rest."

Mom was just getting up when we heard a car turn into our lane. We stopped talking and waited.

Suddenly, we heard January howl. *AaaOooooo!* It was so loud it sounded like he was inside the cabin with us. Then he howled again, and again. *AaaOooooo! AaaOoooooo!* Sure enough. He was doing his "Star Spangled Banner" routine.

Everybody laughed.

"What in the world?" Dad said.

"That's the howl I was telling you about," I said. "Doesn't it sound like he's trying to sing 'The Star Spangled Banner'?"

AaaOooooo!

And then, sure enough, I heard a high, peeling laugh.

Mr. Bennington
Comes Back

AaaOoooooo!

I got up and ran to the door. Dad was right behind me.

Mr. Bennington was standing there, ready to knock. And back next to the pine tree was Mayblossom McDuff. She was still laughing.

AaaOooooo! And January was still howling.

"What's happening?" Mr. Bennington asked.

Dad laughed. "I'm not exactly sure. Maybe Katie knows."

I laughed, too. It was pretty funny.

Mom and Jason joined Dad and me at the door. "Why don't you invite them in?" she suggested.

"See, Mom!" I exclaimed, "I told you she was real!"

M. McDuff laughed even harder.

AaaOooooo!

Mr. Bennington looked amazed. "If showing real estate were always like this, we'd have to sell tickets!" he said.

I figured we'd better start with January. "January, it's OK," I said. "She didn't bite. Remember?"

The stupid dog sat there, his nose still in the air. But he did stop howling. He glanced at M. McDuff. Gradually, he lowered his nose.

"Well, that's better," Dad said. "I think now you can come to the party."

"Delighted," said the smiling face. Her pink jogging shoes eased past the watching dog. She held out her hand to Dad. "I'm M. McDuff."

"This is Steve Hooper," Mr. Bennington said.

"Pleased to meet you," Dad said. "And this is my family—Elizabeth, Jason, and Katie. I guess you already know Katie."

"We met earlier in the week," M. agreed.

"At Flat Rock," I said.

"As a matter of fact, I also met January." M. McDuff's eyes sparkled.

"Don't take it personally," Dad apologized. "He's the dumbest dog we've ever had."

"Well, Katie!" M. smiled extra nice at me. "I certainly never expected to see you today!"

"Same here," I said.

It was Mr. Bennington's turn to speak, and he knew it. "Miss McDuff is vacationing here from the East Coast," he explained. "She's thinking about moving to Colorado."

"If I can find the right cabin," M. said.

"Which brings us to the purpose of our visit," Mr. Bennington continued. "OK if I show her around?"

Dad nodded.

After all the confusion a few minutes before, everything was suddenly quiet. To be honest, I wouldn't have minded if January had begun to howl again. But he didn't. He just lay there, one eye closed, thumping his tail.

"I suppose we might as well finish up in the kitchen," Mom said.

I looked at Jason. He hadn't said a word. He used to talk all the time.

"I can't take a nap until they've seen our bedroom," Mom said.

"Then at least sit down," Dad said. "The rest of us will take care of things."

I don't know if it was just my imagination, but it seemed as if they were upstairs forever. When they finally came back down, M. McDuff was still smiling.

"Your cabin is delightful!" she said. "Are you moving closer to town?"

"This really isn't our cabin," Dad explained.

"We've been renting it."

"I see," she said.

At last they were finished looking. Mom offered them a cup of coffee, but Mr. Bennington said no thanks.

"Do you think we'll be able to leave without a fuss?" he asked. I knew he had to be thinking about January.

"I'll hold the dog," I offered. I ran out and knelt down.

As soon as they came out the door, January howled again! *AaaOooooo!*

I couldn't believe it. "Be still!" I whispered. "This is getting embarrassing."

"Thanks for your kindness," M. said to my family. And she had a special smile for me as she and Mr. Bennington headed for the car.

"I think she's nice," I said. "I can't figure out why January acts like that!"

"It's obvious," Jason said. "He doesn't like her."

I wondered if my brother was right.

Come to think of it, canning peaches turned out to be pretty fatiguing. After we watched them drive away, Dad got out the liver sausage for sandwiches. Mom said she wasn't hungry and went into her room to lie down.

After we ate, Dad, Jason, and I played Monopoly. As usual, in the beginning, it was fun. But at the end, I landed on Boardwalk with three houses on it, which Jason owned, naturally. And Jason said I'd have to pay him, even if I had to mortgage. Well, I could feel my eyes filling with tears. And I hate to be called a baby. So I decided to take my peach pits and go up to my room.

Actually, I never did think of anything to use peach pits for.

* * * * * * * *

When we got home from Sunday school the next day, Mr. Bennington's car was parked in our lane. And January was sitting there howling with his nose in the air. *AaaOoooooo!*

"Are we glad to see you!" Mr. Bennington said. He and M. McDuff were sitting in the front seat of his car.

"I was hoping for another look at the cabin," she said.

Dad smiled. "We'll take January for a walk. Jason, get the leash."

It was January's first time on a leash, and he didn't like it one bit. He sat down in the road and refused to budge.

"Come on, January," I pleaded. He just sat there.

"Let's go, January," Dad said.

Nothing happened.

"We may have to get that dog some training,"

Dad said. "We can't have a dog that won't do what I want."

January must have understood. He stood up and marched off in front of the family.

When we got back from our walk, M. McDuff and Mr. Bennington were still inside the cabin.

"We can't go in," Mom said.

"Of course we can go in," Dad said. "It's still our home."

Jason tied January to the fence, and Dad opened the front door. "We're back," he called.

Mr. Bennington and M. McDuff were sitting in our living room. They both looked very happy.

"I think I've fallen in love!" M. said.

Mr. Bennington looked embarrassed.

"Oh, not with him!" M. grinned. "I never dreamed I could find a cabin with so much charm and personality!"

"Miss McDuff has asked me to call Mr. Allen in California with her purchase offer," Mr. Bennington said. "But she didn't want to leave without telling you first."

"You're buying the cabin?" I asked.

"Yes, Katie," M. said. She was watching me. "You look sad."

"This has been my home all my life," I told her.

"Then you must come back for visits," she insisted. "All of you! I'll be delighted. In fact, I hope you'll come often!"

"When will you be moving in?" Dad asked.

"Not right away," M. said. "Once the deal is final, I'll fly east and put my big house up for sale."

"We'll have to find another place to live," Mom said.

"I'll be glad to help in any way I can," Mr. Bennington offered.

"School starts in a few weeks," Dad said. "I'd like to get the children settled." He glanced at Mom. "And, of course, there's the baby."

"Take your time," M. McDuff said. "Just so I'm in before winter."

"We'll start looking tomorrow," Dad said.

"Mr. Hooper, I have a favor to ask," M. said. "I noticed a sketch of the cabin up in the loft. Could I borrow it to make a copy? I'd like to show my friends."

"Just take it," Dad said. "I'll make Katie another one."

"You've done all the sketches?" she asked.

"I just draw for fun," Dad said. "My real interest is painting mountains."

"Is that right?" Mr. Bennington said. "We've been admiring all the art."

"Of course!" M. McDuff said. "*You* must be the artist! I saw your painting in the bank!"

Dad smiled.

Then Mr. Bennington stood up. "I think we'd

better get to a telephone," he said.

As I watched them walk out the door, I felt kind of numb. Mom looked as if she might cry. Dad patted her hand. And Jason climbed the ladder to the loft.

Dad sighed. "I wonder what the M. stands for?" he said.

"It's Mayblossom, " I told him. "She was named for a tap dancing teacher."

And then January howled. *AaaOooooo!* Only once. Then they were gone.

We Begin Cabin Hunting

Dad took a long look at Mom. Then, nodding his head, he smiled. "'The Lord gave, and the Lord has taken away,'" he quoted from the Bible.

Mom smiled back and finished the verse: "'May the name of the Lord be praised.'"

"What will happen now?" I asked.

"We don't know," Dad said.

"But the Lord does," Mom finished. And I could tell that Dad agreed.

He smiled at me. "Katie, please help your mother set the table."

It was good to have something to do. I concentrated on putting each knife and fork and spoon exactly parallel.

While Mom sat at the sink cleaning berries, she started singing, "Blessed be the Lord—for His great mercy." Although I didn't know all the words, pretty soon I joined in.

Well, Mom and I ended up singing the entire time we were getting dinner ready. And it helped. I felt happy. And I didn't feel scared.

Later, when we had all gathered around the table, Dad reminded us to think about what we were singing: "Praise God, from whom all blessings flow!" It had special meaning for us today.

We sat down. "But why would God take the cabin away from us?" Jason asked. "He must know how much we love the land."

"We shouldn't ask *why*," Dad told us. "Sometimes the Lord tells us why things happen. But often He does not."

"I believe the Lord has something special for us," Mom said.

"Well, at least we can come back here for visits," I remembered.

"And we can be thankful the land won't be turned into condos," Jason said. "I think that Ms. Morganstern planned to bulldoze the cabin."

"Only the Lord can see the big picture," Dad said. "He wants us to trust Him. That's the lesson we must keep learning."

Faith in God must be "catching"! By the time we got to devotions, I was actually starting to get excited about where we'd live next. In fact, we all were. Even Jason.

"Lord, we won't try to tell you what our next home should be like," Dad prayed. "We trust You to give us what You think best!"

"Please, Jesus, just show us where it is," Mom prayed.

"I've been asking You for a friend," I told the Lord. "Do You have a home with neighbors?"

"No offense," Jason prayed, "but, Lord, we don't have forever!"

After prayers, we stayed at the table to work out plans for the next morning.

"I think I should go to work," Jason said. "The Cochrans are counting on me to help with the sheep."

"Your responsibility there comes first," Dad agreed. "Why don't you ask Cochrans if they know of property for rent?"

"OK," Jason said. "I bet if there's any land around here, Cochrans will know about it."

Dad looked at Mom. "We could be riding around in Purple Jeep a long time tomorrow," he said. "Maybe I should just take Katie. She and I can narrow down the choices. Then we can pick you up so you can make the final decision."

"That sounds good to me." Mom smiled.

* * * * * * * *

During the night I dreamed we rented a wonderful cabin by a stream so Dad could fish every day. As it turned out, we never even saw the place.

When Dad and I finished breakfast, Mom was still in bed. We were very quiet.

"Shall we take January?" I wondered.

Dad thought a minute. "Sure," he said. "Why not? He might bring us luck."

On the way out, the door squeaked. And Dad forgot his hat and had to go back. But, finally, we were ready for our adventure. January jumped into the back seat of Purple Jeep and sat there with his tongue hanging out.

"Let's hit the trail!" Dad said. At the end of the lane, he turned left. Soon we were rattling down the unpaved road.

"Katie, would you like to live close enough to Flat Rock that you could walk?" Dad asked.

My heart sank. "That might be nice," I said.

"I've been thinking," he continued. "If we lived closer, I could paint that morning light on the mountain in every season."

So, for a little while, it sounded as if I might get even better acquainted with my dolls. Hello Audrey and B. B. and Gomer! And goodbye real friends!

"You watch that side of the road for FOR RENT signs," Dad said. "I'll watch this side."

But the only sign we saw all morning said, "24 miles to Good Food."

"This doesn't look promising," Dad admitted. "Maybe we'd better find a town and buy a newspaper."

We soon discovered that the sign was wrong. It might have been 24 miles, but it sure wasn't Good Food. Dad said as long as we had to go into the restaurant anyway, we might as well eat. And then they didn't even have a newspaper.

"Do you know of any places to rent?" Dad asked the waitress.

"What kind of places?" she asked. A button pinned onto her dress said, *Hilda.*

"You know," Dad said. "Like a cabin?"

"Why didn't you say so?" she said. She turned and yelled, "Joe!"

After lunch, Dad followed Joe, and I followed Dad. And January followed me.

"You can take your pick," Joe said. "This time of year, I have lots of vacancies." There were five tiny yellow cabins with matching peeling paint. Joe opened the door of the first one.

"Needs a little airing out, that's all," Joe said.

Dad and I looked at the painted iron bed and the rose chenille bedspread hung over the top of a sagging mattress. Through the only door I could see a dirty bathroom.

"I'm sorry," Dad said. "I need something much

110

bigger. Something more permanent."

"Suit yourself," Joe said. He turned on his heel.

I thought I might start to giggle, so I didn't even look at Dad.

When we got back to Purple Jeep, January curled up in the back seat. And Dad turned the car in the other direction. "This isn't going to be as easy as I thought," he said.

"Maybe Mr. Bennington could help us," I suggested.

"He's way up in Denver," Dad said. "I guess we could get help from a real estate person in Woodland Park. I think there's one next door to the bank."

Traffic picked up as we approached the bigger town. And January started to snore. Dad parked Purple Jeep. "First, I think I'll pick up a newspaper," he said.

I was just sitting in the car waiting. Suddenly, somebody on the sidewalk pointed. And then lots of people came crowding around.

"Isn't that the car?" a girl asked.

"It's him! It's the dog!" somebody said. "In the back seat!"

"Sure enough!"

Everybody was peering in at January. And January was just snoring away like nothing at all was happening. I couldn't believe it.

"What's going on?" Dad asked, returning with the paper.

"It's the dog who eats ice cream cones!" a little boy told him.

"Look at your newspaper," a man said.

Well, that's how we found out that January had become famous! There, on the front page, right in the middle, was a picture of my dog! January was eating an ice cream cone!

Actually, that turned out to be the best part of the whole day. All the tourists stopped to gape at the dog who eats ice cream cones. Naturally, January woke up. He looked from one person to the next, and then he started to whine.

Dad left me to babysit January while he went into the real estate office. Maybe he thought I'd have fun. But during the whole time Dad was gone, nobody said a word to me. All they cared about was January.

When Dad came back out, he didn't look very happy. "It looks bad," he said. "The realtor asked if I didn't know this is tourist country. People who want to rent their places get lots of money from out-of-state visitors."

"You mean, he doesn't have any cabins for us to look at?" I asked. "Not even one?"

"Nothing," Dad said. "He took my phone number. If something turns up, he'll call us."

I hate it when Dad looks sad. "I have an idea,"

I said. "Let's go in the bank and visit your paint-ing."

"You go, Katie," he said. "I'll babysit the super-star." He looked at January.

What I hoped was that Dad's painting would have a sign on it that said, SOLD. Or that the stone wall in the bank would be bare.

But what really happened was that the paint-ing was still hanging there, right where it was before. And nobody was even looking at it.

January Ruins Everything

Although we didn't plan it on the way home, somehow I knew that at supper we'd be telling Mom and Jason only about all the funny things that happened.

"I didn't even think about it at the time," Dad said at supper. "Maybe we could have rented all five of the little yellow cabins!"

"One for each of us," laughed Mom. "Even one for the baby."

"She could have the pink bedspread," I said. "Unless, of course, we have a boy!"

"You should have seen it!" Dad laughed. "It reminded me of an old bathrobe my grandmother used to wear."

"Well, at least we know there's no house for us

to rent in that part of the country," Mom said.

"I asked Mr. Cochran if he knew of any places," Jason reported. "Unfortunately, we're too late. There used to be a forty-acre spread near the Springs. For a long time, it just sat there. Then, finally, Mr. Cochran bought it himself. His son's turning it into a guest ranch."

"I just can't believe the prices," Dad sighed. "It's hard to believe what's happening to the cost of real estate around here."

"It makes those prices fifteen years ago seem almost like a give-away," Mom remembered.

"It's too bad you didn't buy some land then," Jason said.

"We didn't have money then," Dad said. "I have no regrets. That kind of thinking just leads to bitterness!" He nodded to me. "Katie, did you tell them we have a celebrity in the family?"

That signaled my turn to tell about January. Afterwards, I showed them the newspaper. "Doesn't January look cute?"

"I'm not sure *cute* is the word to describe January," Jason said. He grinned.

"Maybe somebody will see January's picture and hear about us needing a place to live," Mom said. "The Lord has His ways."

Dad didn't respond.

"After all, this is only the first day," Mom continued.

116

After supper, we prayed again for a place to live. If anyone felt discouraged, no one said so.

But by the end of the third day, everything was still the same. Except that Dad and I stopped riding around looking for places with FOR RENT signs. On Thursday, he took off alone in Purple Jeep, with his paints.

"What will happen to us?" I asked Mom.

"The Lord will provide something," she said. "He loves us. And He knows our needs."

"Maybe I shouldn't have prayed for a friend," I said. "That's probably made finding a place a lot harder."

Mom laughed out loud. "Nonsense," she said. "Nothing's too hard for the Lord."

I was glad to hear her say that.

* * * * * * * *

On Thursday night, while we were eating supper, the telephone rang.

"I'll get it," Dad said.

"Four bedrooms?" we heard Dad ask.

I watched Mom's face turn into a huge smile.

But Dad wasn't smiling. He kept nodding his head. "Well," he said, "thanks for letting me know. We'll certainly consider it. I'll call you back."

"What's happening?" Jason asked.

"It was the realtor next to the bank," Dad said. "He has a house for rent across from the middle school."

"You don't seem enthusiastic," Mom noticed.

"It doesn't have any land," Dad said. "It's just a small city lot."

"Steve, we really can't expect a cabin on 50 acres," Mom pointed out.

"It's across from my school?" I asked.

"You did say it has four bedrooms, didn't you?" Mom remembered.

"OK, let's go see it," Dad said.

Dad called the realtor and arranged for us to meet him at the house. Then we all piled into Purple Jeep, even January, who took his place in the back seat between Jason and me. He promptly laid down. Before we were even out of the lane, he was asleep.

"See!" I told my brother. "I told you he snores! I think being famous must be very fatiguing."

But Jason wasn't even listening.

We parked by the school and sat there looking at the house. The outside was painted tan. It looked exactly like the houses on both sides, except one of them was blue and the other was green.

"It seems to be in good condition," Mom said.

Dad opened the door. "Let's go in."

We formed a funny parade. First Dad, loping

118

along with his green golf hat on. Then Mom, waddling along in her blue tent dress. Then Jason, swaggering along, looking cool. And then me, looking (I guess) exactly like I always look.

Just as Dad pushed the doorbell, the front door opened, and a smiling man invited us in. "Mr. Hooper, you're in luck," he said. "Just yesterday, the Cantrells were told to report to Chanute Field in Illinois."

Well, we could see right away that the house isn't one bit like our cabin. When you first walk in, you have to decide whether you want to go upstairs or downstairs. The smiling man led the way up.

"Notice the mountain view from the dining area," he said. We noticed. You kind of had to look around a roof and a chimney, but the smiling man was right.

"Brand new, first-quality carpeting," the smiling man said. Mom noticed and smiled, also.

"And here we have the modern, efficient kitchen," the smiling man said. We took turns leaning into the doorway and looking. I was glad our peaches were all canned.

"Two bedrooms-and-a-bath up, and another two bedrooms-and-a-bath down," the smiling man said. So far, we had only seen up, but we took his word for it.

While the smiling man led the way downstairs, I heard Mom whisper to Dad, "It's nice and clean."

"Katie and I could sleep down here," Jason said. "Hey, we'd even have our own bathroom!" In the cabin we all have to take turns.

All this time, Dad hadn't said a word, The salesman stopped looking at him and concentrated on Mom. "The Cantrells fixed this place up for themselves," he said. "Now they expect to come back here when they retire."

"How much is the rent?" Dad asked.

"The most important thing to the Cantrells is having tenants who will take good care of everything." The smiling man reached into his pocket for a piece of paper. He read off a number.

I watched Dad's face. He didn't wince, which was a good sign. "When could we move in?" he asked.

"Actually, you can have the house tomorrow," the smiling man said. "The Cantrells' things will be picked up in the morning. That's the air force for you."

Dad looked at Mom. "I suppose I could plant a garden out in back," he said. "I think I'll check out the yard."

As Dad went out the door, we heard barking.

"Oh, no," I said. "January woke up."

The man stopped smiling. "You don't have a dog, do you?"

I nodded. I didn't know what else to do.

"He's very well ... trained." Mom searched for the right word. "What I mean is, he's not always smart, but he's never ruined anything."

"I'm sorry," the man said. "The Cantrells were very firm. They have just spent a lot of money fixing up this house. They will not allow animals."

"But January is a special dog," I explained. "Maybe you saw his picture in the paper?"

The man just looked at me. He did not smile.

While we were all standing there, Dad walked back in. "Well," he said, "what's wrong?"

The man never smiled now. "Mr. Hooper, I understand you have a dog," the man said. "I'm very sorry. The Cantrells will not rent this house to anyone with animals."

At first Dad didn't say a word. "Well, I guess that does it," he said softly. "Come on, Elizabeth. Let's go."

We followed Dad out to Purple Jeep and the barking January. Only by then the dog had stopped barking. Now he was kind of whistling.

"If only January hadn't barked," I moaned.

"It's their house," Dad said. "The owners have a right to exclude dogs."

Everybody was quiet. We all climbed back into Purple Jeep. Dad started the motor.

"Even if we wanted to, we never could have

121

hidden a dog like January," Mom said.

"In the Bible story, they hid Moses in the bull-rushes," I remembered.

"That was different," Dad said.

"Right," added Jason. "Moses didn't howl."

Good News for Dad

"Maybe this afternoon I can take you to the library," Mom told me. "If Dad gets home in time."

It was Friday morning. Dad was just loading his paints into Purple Jeep when the telephone rang.

"It's for you, Steve," Mom said.

"No, Chuck, not yet," we heard Dad say. Then for a long time he just listened. "I understand," he said, finally. "I'll talk it over with my wife and let you know. And thank you for thinking of me." He hung up the phone.

"Who was that?" Mom wondered.

"It was Chuck Cochran at the sheep ranch. You know, Jason's boss," Dad said. "Elizabeth, I

123

think you'd better sit down."

Mom poured them each a cup of coffee.

I wasn't sure if this was private or not. "OK if I stick around?" I asked.

"It's all right, Katie," Dad said. "This concerns the whole family."

"Well?" Mom asked.

"I hardly know where to begin," Dad said. "Remember a few nights ago, when Jason told us about the forty acres near the Springs? The land Chuck bought? His oldest son is developing it as a guest ranch."

"I remember," Mom said.

"You won't believe this." Dad looked at Mom. "They want me to run it," he told her.

"You're kidding!" Mom set her cup on the coffee table. On top of the newspapers.

"Actually, Cochrans thought we owned our land here," Dad continued. "I guess they were really surprised when Jason told them we need a place to live."

"That's probably because we were already living here when they bought their ranch and decided to raise sheep," Mom said.

"I suppose," Dad said. "Anyhow, their son's plan is to attract tourists with children to the guest ranch. They'd like to make it a family vacation spot. And they're excited about the idea of having a family living there year-round."

"Namely, us!" Mom said. She was smiling. "It might be fun. All of us could pitch in and help. It would be great for Jason and Katie!"

"What do you think, Katie?" Dad asked.

"It sounds like a wonderful adventure," I said. "Would we have to go to school?" Mom and Dad laughed.

"Is there a house there for us?" Mom asked.

"There is," Dad smiled. "In fact, it sounds like a nice one," Dad told her. "And they'd pay us a generous salary besides."

"Oh, Steve, isn't the Lord good!" Mom said. She was smiling from ear to ear!

But then Dad stopped smiling. "There's only one trouble," he said. Mom and I looked at him. I tried to think of what it could be.

"The offer does sound tempting," Dad said. "But, I just remembered that I don't know a thing about horses! In fact, none of us knows a thing about horses. Elizabeth, I don't even *like* horses!"

Then Mom stopped smiling. "I guess that would be a problem," she said slowly.

"And, in the second place," Dad continued, "if we had responsibility for guests at the ranch, I doubt if I'd have much time to use my artistic talents. And, after all, I came out to Colorado to paint mountains."

"That's true," Mom agreed slowly.

Before my very eyes, I could see a wonderful new adventure disappearing!

"But, Steve, maybe we should at least pray about it," Mom said.

Dad looked at her. "Of course, you're right, Elizabeth," he said. "I'm sorry. You know, I'm not always thinking clearly these days. It's so hard for me to see you feeling insecure. I mean, with the baby and everything."

"Actually, I don't feel insecure," Mom assured him. "I know the Lord has plans for us."

"Elizabeth, I love you very much!"

"And I love you, Steve," Mom told him softly.

I could have felt like an intruder, but the truth is I didn't. Still, it was one of those times when my parents didn't even remember I was there.

I couldn't help notice that their prayers sounded just like they do when we pray every night. I mean, it wasn't a big deal. Mom prayed that the Lord would give us a place to live. And Dad prayed that the Lord would show them if he was supposed to manage the guest ranch. "Just tell me what You want, Lord," he prayed. "You know I'll do it!"

The the mailman blew his horn, and I ran down the lane to where he waited in his car.

"Hi," I called.

"Katie, I have a package for you," he said. "And a letter for your father." He handed me a bundle of stuff with a string around it.

"Thanks," I told him.

"Say," he said, "I saw January's picture in the newspaper. How does he like being famous?"

I laughed. "So far, he's just acted tired!"

"If you ever want to sell him, let me know!" he said. "I've been wanting another dog."

"OK," I told him. I walked back to the cabin wondering if Dad had ever thought about getting rid of January. It was the first time such an idea ever entered my head.

When I got inside, I untied the string and looked at the package. "It's from Mayblossom McDuff!" I said. I tried to pull open the fat, brown package, but little dusty stuff flew all over.

"It's a book bag," Mom said. "Stand still, Katie, or you'll get that all over the cabin!"

With Mom's help, we finally pulled out two books. "Just what I needed," I said. "I wonder how M. knew I was out of books?" Immediately, I sat down on the couch and opened the first one.

Mom held up the other book. "Steve, look at this," she said. "It says, *by M. McDuff.* M. McDuff writes books!"

I stopped reading and looked at the cover of my book. "This one has her name on it, too!" I said.

"Well, imagine that," Mom said. "Our cabin

belongs to a real-live author!"

Dad wasn't paying attention. He had opened his letter and had started reading it. "Elizabeth!" he said. "Wait until you hear this!"

"What is it?" Mom asked.

"Just a minute," he said. "I'll tell you in a minute." His eyes sparkled. "I think it's an answer to our prayer!"

Well, nobody could concentrate on reading with all that going on! So I closed my book. I slid my fingers across the author's name. I wondered if anyone else knew what the M. stands for?

"This is a letter from the publisher of M. McDuff's books," Dad said. "They want to know if I'd be interested in illustrating children's books. I wonder how they happened to write to me?"

"I bet I know," I said. "Remember the drawings you gave to M.? The sketch of the cabin?"

"You're right, Katie." Dad read on. "They like the way I draw. They'll pay me for drawing! Why, the funny thing is that I've never even considered trying to sell my sketches!"

"Well, it isn't exactly painting," Mom said. "But you would be using the talent God gave you!"

"The sketching goes so fast," Dad said. "I'd still have lots of time to paint!"

Dad pulled Mom to her feet. They started hugging each other and dancing around. Well, with

Mom's shape, it wasn't exactly hugging, and it wasn't exactly dancing. But I've never seen my parents so happy!

"It's a miracle," Mom said.

"Somehow I didn't think I was supposed to take care of horses!" Dad laughed. "But I meant it when I told God I was willing!"

And just when I thought the day had to be the most exciting one in my entire life, the telephone rang again. I answered. The caller was another man who also wanted to talk to Dad.

By then, Dad was really acting silly. He galloped his huge body all the way over to the telephone. Mom and I just watched and laughed. Finally, he took the phone.

"Steve Hooper here," he said, still laughing. "Oh, hi, Harry!" Then Dad quieted down and started to listen. "Harry, that's wonderful!" he said. "How about if I come down right after lunch?"

Mom couldn't believe it. "Now what?" she asked.

Dad hung up the telephone. "Wait until you hear this, Elizabeth!" he said. And then, while we watched, a strange thing happened. Dad's eyes were filling with tears.

"Steve, what's wrong?" Mom asked.

My father could hardly speak. "It was Harry," he said. "Harry Upjohn at the bank." He blinked. "Someone has bought my mountain painting!"

"Praise the Lord!" Mom said softly.

"Well, that should take care of the doctor bill!" Dad said.

"I hardly know what to say." Mom's voice was quiet. "I know the Lord cares about us, but today is almost too much to take in!"

Later, we all calmed down enough to eat liver sausage sandwiches for lunch. But while my father was fishing for a sweet pickle, he suddenly thought of something.

"The Lord still has one problem left," Dad remembered. "I nearly forgot. We still need a place to live!"

A Home for Hoopers

My parents never stopped smiling the whole time we rode to town.

"Steve, I'm so proud of you," Mom said.

"Some wives wouldn't have had enough faith to stick it out," Dad said. "And, don't forget, you still don't have a roof over your head." But he was smiling when he said it.

"You know, I'm really not worried about it," Mom told him. "I just know something will turn up."

"The strange thing is that I know it, too," Dad agreed. "I wonder where it will be?"

In the back seat, next to me, January snored.

"The mailman offered to buy January," I said. "I forgot to tell you."

"That's ridiculous," Dad said. "That dog's a vital part of the family."

"Yes," Mom added. "He makes us laugh!"

January was still asleep when Dad parked the car in front of the bank. "Can we leave him alone?" I asked.

"We shouldn't be long," Dad said. "I guess all he can do is bark. And there's no way he can ruin things today."

When I glanced up at the stone wall, the painting was gone. "It looks bare," I told my father. "You'll have to paint another one."

"Maybe you should take off your hat," Mom suggested.

"Nonsense." My father grinned.

We followed Dad past all the tellers and into a small office at the end. When the man at the desk saw us, he stood up and held out his hand. "Congratulations, Steve," he said.

"Meet the world's best encourager," Dad said. "This is Harry Upjohn. Harry, this is my wife, Elizabeth, and my daughter, Katie."

Mr. Upjohn has the biggest smile I've ever seen. And the baldest head. "The Lord hasn't given me a lot of talent," he said, "but I can applaud those who do have it!" He turned to me. "And, Katie, your father has marvelous talent!"

Suddenly, I felt all warm and tingling. I was very glad I hadn't waited in the car. I smiled. "I

133

think it's my father's best painting," I agreed. "I went with him the morning he painted it."

"It's no wonder the Cantrells haven't been able to get that mountain out of their minds!" Mr. Upjohn said. "They called me all the way from Illinois this morning."

"Is he in the air force?" Dad asked.

Mr. Upjohn looked surprised. "Do you know him?"

"I think we looked at his house last night," Mom said. "Across from the school?"

"That's the couple," Mr. Upjohn said. "At first, they passed up the painting because they were leaving town. But then they became almost frantic at the thought of someone else buying it! I had to promise them I'd take it right off the wall."

"We prayed that the right people would buy it," Dad said.

"The Cantrells are the right people, Steve," Mr. Upjohn said. "They love the painting. And right now they really need to feel God's love."

"To be honest, I wasn't sure anybody would pay that much for it," Dad said.

"Nonsense," Mr. Upjohn said. "They wired the money immediately. He opened his desk drawer. "Here you go, Steve," he said. "Or maybe I should give the check to your wife!" He laughed.

"It doesn't matter," Mom said. "Either way, it's

earmarked for doctor bills!"

"It looks like it won't be long." Mr. Upjohn looked at Mom's shape and smiled. "But, Steve, I didn't know you were planning to move."

"Our cabin was just sold," Dad explained. "An author bought it."

"Not Mayblossom McDuff!" Mr. Upjohn said. When Dad nodded, he continued. "She was here in the bank last week. We gave her the name of a realtor in Denver."

"It's a small world after all," Dad said. "I really can't believe my painting was sold to the Cantrells. We looked at their house just last night."

"They told me their house is special," Mr. Upjohn said. "They sure hated to leave it."

"It's a nice house all right," Mom agreed. "Unfortunately for us, they don't want renters with pets. And we have a dog."

"So ..." Mr. Upjohn paused. "Have you found something else?"

"There's not much to find," Dad told him. "I really don't know what we'll do."

"I wish I could help you," Mr. Upjohn said. "I don't know of any other rentals in town."

"How about out of town?" Mom asked. She smiled. "Any old manger will do."

Harry laughed. "Well, there is one possibility, but it would never do."

"Try us," Dad said.

"You've heard of *Rent-A-Wreck?*" Harry asked. "Well, usually it refers to a car!" He laughed at his own joke.

"Harry, tell us about it," Dad said.

"You're serious?"

Dad and Mom both nodded.

"Well, there's this place south of town. It was just abandoned last year. The bank owns the land. Frankly, we figured some developer would just level the house and build something good on the property. But so far we've had no takers."

"Would you rent it?" Mom asked.

"It really isn't something you'd want to put a family in, Elizabeth," Mr. Upjohn said.

"Maybe we could fix it up," Dad said. "We have a little time before we have to move."

"You really are serious, aren't you?" Mr. Upjohn nodded his bald head.

"Can you take us to see it?" Mom asked.

* * * * * * * *

Purple Jeep followed Mr. Upjohn's shining gold car through town and past the school.

Dad and Mom were laughing. "Are people looking at us? I feel like a poor relative," she said.

"You aren't poor any longer, Mrs. Hooper," Dad reminded her.

South of town, Mr. Upjohn's car turned off the highway. He waited until Purple Jeep followed.

"It's pretty close to the school," Dad said.

Mr. Upjohn pulled to the side of the road, and Dad parked behind him. We got out and stood together looking.

Mr. Upjohn was right. The house *is* a wreck.

It stood there, big and ugly. I'm not even sure what color it was supposed to be. The door and the downstairs windows were all boarded up. And another of the windows upstairs should have been. A green curtain flapped out through broken glass.

"I told you it wasn't a good place for a family," Mr. Upjohn said. "Now you can see what I mean."

"Nobody lives there?" Dad asked.

"It's been vacant for over a year. I expect if those walls could talk they'd have quite a story to tell!" Mr. Upjohn said.

Mom giggled. "The truth is, I've always wanted to live in a Victorian house."

"Oh, it's Victorian, all right." Mr. Upjohn laughed.

We just stood there. Nobody said anything. Then, in the car, January whined.

"Of course, it would cost something to fix the place up," Dad said.

"Not a whole lot," Mr. Upjohn said. "And the

bank would lend the money." He looked serious. "Frankly, the insurance costs for vacant property are killing us. The bank would be happy to get out from under what the place is costing us!"

"How much would it rent for?" Dad asked.

"You could probably have it for nothing," Mr. Upjohn said.

"You're kidding!" Mom said.

"Well, you'd have to pay insurance and taxes," Mr. Upjohn said.

I watched Mom's face. She was starting to look excited.

In fact, Dad was starting to look excited.

And I suppose, if the truth were known, *I* was even starting to look excited.

"Harry," Dad said, holding out his hand, "I think you just got yourself a deal!"

Something for Me

"What have we done?" Dad said, when we got back to the cabin.

"We've found our new home!" Mom reminded him. I don't think he needed reminding.

"You haven't said much, Katie." Dad looked at me. "What are you thinking?"

"The whole thing reminds me of an adventure," I told him. "Something that happens in a book. How come real people never have adventures?"

"Sometimes real people do," Mom said. "If they're willing to take a chance!" She grinned at Dad.

"Your mother sounds exactly like she did when I married her!" Dad said. "Elizabeth,

139

you're something special!" he told her.

When Jason got home, all of us were talking at once.

"It sounds as if I missed out on everything," my brother said. "Here I thought it was just an ordinary day!"

"Would you like to take a drive down to see the house?" Dad asked. "I'll even buy ice cream cones to celebrate."

"Let's go!" Jason said.

I couldn't believe it. We didn't even stop to eat supper. Mom just turned off the stove and left everything!

* * * * * * * *

Although we had told Jason all about the house, I could tell he was surprised. "Wow!" he said. "It's huge! It must have a millions rooms!"

"Not quite a million," Mom laughed. "And only one bathroom."

"Oh, well. We aren't used to more than one bathroom," Jason said. "Can we go inside?"

"Not yet," Dad told him. "We have to work out the insurance and a few other details."

"We could walk around a little," Mom said.

This time, when we got out of the car, January started barking. "Be still!" I said. But he wouldn't stop.

"I'd rather not have him tearing around the property," Dad said. "Not yet."

"I'll stay with him," I offered. "I got to walk around this afternoon."

I watched my family go. "Well, January, are you ready for adventure?" I asked.

He just looked at me.

"It's getting hard to know what will happen next," I said.

Well, I was right. It *was* hard to know. Suddenly, January pointed his nose in the air and started to howl! *AaaOooooo!* It was his "Star Spangled Banner" routine. And, this time, I knew Mayblossom McDuff was nowhere around!

And then a face appeared at Purple Jeep's window!

I screamed.

"I'm sorry," the girl said. "I didn't mean to scare you!"

"Well, you did scare me," I told her. "Don't you know you shouldn't sneak up on people like that?"

"I wasn't sneaking," the girl said. "I live over there. I just wanted to get a better look at this purple car."

"It's Purple Jeep," I said. "And you might as well get used to it. As soon as we get the place fixed up a little, we're moving here."

"You're kidding!" she said.

"No, I'm not," I told her. "My name is Katie Hooper."

"And I'm Sara Wilcox," she said. "I still can't believe it."

"It might look like a wreck to you," I said loyally. "But my mother says the place is a beautiful Victorian lady in disguise."

"Oh, I wasn't surprised about the house," Sara said. "I was surprised about you. Ever since I moved here this summer, I have been praying for a friend." She smiled. "What took you so long?"

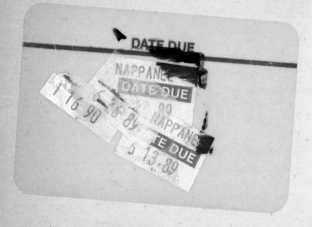